S0-BNH-794

More praise for Stuart Kaminsky and LIEBERMAN'S THIEF

"Kaminsky gets more subplots going than I would have imagined possible in 198 pages, but in the end he gracefully combines the stories of a stupendously varied cast of characters."
—*The Washington Post Book World*

"[An] entertaining tale . . . Kaminsky draws each [character] with such succinct deftness any of them could have sufficed as a protagonist in a lesser man's novel."
—*Richmond Times-Dispatch*

"Highly recommended . . . Kaminsky captures the sights and sounds of his Chicago setting most convincingly. He guides us through the police-procedural aspects of the plot smoothly, while depicting enough of Lieberman's and Hanrahan's personal lives to make them fully realized characters. . . . He consistently creates interesting plots and believable characters."
—*Booklist*

"Nobody writing today can mix taut suspense with a sense of creeping mortality as shatteringly as Kaminsky."
—*Kirkus Reviews*

By Stuart Kaminsky:

THE DEVIL MET A LADY
THE MELTING CLOCK
POOR BUTTERFLY
BURIED CAESARS
THINK FAST, MR. PETERS
SMART MOVES
THE MAN WHO SHOT LEWIS VANCE
DOWN FOR THE COUNT
THE FALA FACTOR
HE DONE HER WRONG
CATCH A FALLING CLOWN
HIGH MIDNIGHT
NEVER CROSS A VAMPIRE
THE HOWARD HUGHES AFFAIR
YOU BET YOUR LIFE
MURDER ON THE YELLOW BRICK ROAD
BULLET FOR A STAR
WHEN THE DARK MAN CALLS
EXERCISE IN TERROR

Abe Lieberman Mysteries:
LIEBERMAN'S FOLLY*
LIEBERMAN'S CHOICE*
LIEBERMAN'S DAY*
LIEBERMAN'S THIEF*

Inspector Rostnikov Mysteries:
A FINE RED RAIN*
DEATH OF A DISSIDENT*
BLACK KNIGHT IN RED SQUARE*
A COLD RED SUNRISE*
RED CHAMELEON*
ROSTNIKOV'S VACATION*
THE MAN WHO WALKED LIKE A BEAR*
DEATH OF A RUSSIAN PRIEST*
HARD CURRENCY*
BLOOD AND RUBLES*

Published by Fawcett/Ivy Books

Books published by The Ballantine Publishing Group
are available at quantity discounts on bulk purchases
for premium, educational, fund-raising, and special
sales use. For details, please call 1-800-733-3000.

LIEBERMAN'S THIEF

Stuart Kaminsky

IVY BOOKS • NEW YORK

Sale of this book without a front cover may be unauthorized. If this book is coverless, it may have been reported to the publisher as "unsold or destroyed" and neither the author nor the publisher may have received payment for it.

Ivy Books
Published by Ballantine Books
Copyright © 1995 by Stuart Kaminsky

All rights reserved under International and Pan-American Copyright Conventions. Published in the United States by Ballantine Books, a division of Random House, Inc., New York, and distributed in Canada by Random House of Canada Limited, Toronto.

Library of Congress Catalog Card Number: 95-94967

ISBN 0-8041-1287-8

This edition published by arrangement with Henry Holt and Company

Manufactured in the United States of America

First Ballantine Books Edition: March 1996

10 9 8 7 6 5 4 3 2

To Bernard Feinberg, M.D.,
and Elliott Livstone, M.D.,
with thanks for keeping
the ship afloat

"For here, among my friends I learnt to measure
your mind, your menace, and your enmity.
But if I had been trapped inside your house,
you would have sent me straight to death."
—ION IN *ION*, BY EURIPIDES

The Burglar Prowls

George Patniks hated his nickname, "Pitty-Pitty." There was no dignity in a name like Pitty-Pitty Patniks, but then Alex Sewell, the boss of cell block C, hadn't been concerned about George's dignity. Sewell had a great nickname, "Steelhead." It implied that nothing could penetrate Sewell's head, not a tool shop knife made from a toothbrush, not a V bar loosened from the bottom of a bunk, not a thought or idea. Steelhead was a risky nickname. It gave a target and defied the other cons to go after it.

But Pitty-Pitty, what the hell sense did that make? George, whose real name was Gregor Eupatniaks, was sure that Steelhead Sewell, who was serving two life sentences for murdering a pair of runaway girls in Moline, hadn't thought about the nickname he bestowed on the skinny kid who had just done the first month of time for his first felony, breaking and entering.

But the name stuck. George couldn't shake it. It followed him to Chicago's Near North Side neighborhood where he had spent his life, except for the two years he had done for breaking and entering and the two more years he had done for breaking and entering again and the year he had done for possession of a weapon, a dinky piece, a .22 he carried in his tool belt under his jacket. It was really the burglary tools in the belt that they had gotten him for, not the Friday night nothing-special, but they couldn't nail him on the tools so they got him for the gun.

Even the police called him Pitty-Pitty. A grown man, now pushing forty-six, with almost six years of down time on three felonies. That was one of the worst things about

1

being picked up, cops yelling his nickname across a squad room.

George considered himself one of the most successful burglars in Cook County. He wasn't sure how many houses, businesses, and apartments he had plucked—two hundred? Maybe three hundred? Maybe more? You'd think he'd keep count, but he didn't, like a movie star on Jay Leno who can't remember how many movies he's been in.

George hadn't worked an honest day in his life since his sixteenth birthday, but the dishonest ones had added up over the years. He practiced his profession once every three or four weeks for a few hours—not counting set-up time—and devoted the rest of his time to eating, sleeping, hanging out with his brother when he was around, and trying, sometimes successfully, to pick up women or girls at Unikle's Tap or the Blue Truck Bar. But what he liked to do most was something that he had picked up in prison. George's passion was painting. He had always liked to draw, but in prison an artist from Chicago named Joplin—guy in denims, hair hanging over his eyes, mess of a beard—had conducted a six-week class in painting. George had taken to it. He was a natural. He could paint what was in his head from the moment he picked up the brush.

Most people thought Steelhead Sewell had given him the name Pitty-Pitty because it was what Steelhead thought it sounded like when George was painting. Trouble was, George was sure Steelhead Sewell did not know he was taking the class or painting.

Joplin the painter had told George that he had talent. Years later, when George was exhibiting in an art fair in Lincoln Park, he ran into Joplin, who was showing his own stuff. They talked. Joplin said he had been out of town a few years. His hands shook. Rummy. Joplin's paintings were for shit. Who had he been to tell George Patniks that he was a good painter? George had a better grasp on reality than that.

George looked at his own paintings—cons leaning lonelily against concrete block walls, smoking and looking at nothing, buildings that looked so tired they might tumble

2

over with a pat on the back from a good wind off Lake Michigan, kids playing in the park on the merry-go-round but not looking like they were having fun. George knew he had the eye. But he didn't have the magic. Wasn't there. No avoiding the truth. No use crying. George could paint. He could paint what he saw, but he was never going to be anything but a summer exhibitor looking for a park district ribbon.

That was fine with George. No kicks. Life was good. Work once every couple of weeks. Make the good score, sometimes big cash in the back of a drawer inside a pair of socks. Sometimes a good sale to one of the pawnshops on Devon or Milwaukee that fenced on the back and down side. You get caught once in a now and then. That was the price. You took it straight up. It was usually bad luck that got you. At least it had been bad luck that got George each time he had been caught, a really good silent alarm connected to a security service, neighbors when there shouldn't have been, a small green-stoned necklace hidden under the floorboard of his apartment and lucked on by an overeager detective on his first case.

But George was older now. A lot older. He had learned from his mistakes. He never talked about his jobs. He cased each one far beyond what any pro might consider reasonable. He'd get the book hard and heavy and not across his knuckles the next time he stood before a judge with decent evidence on the table. George had to be careful.

He pulled out his wallet and extracted the sheet of paper on which he had written a phone number. Then he dialed the number. It rang four times. Music in the background. Classical. George recognized it but couldn't give a name.

"Good evening," the woman said softly.

"Mr. Harvey Rozier," George said, disguising his voice by going an octave higher and a bit slower and more precise than his normal. "Or Mrs. Rozier."

"The concert is about to begin," the woman said.

"Very important," George insisted. "Mr. Rozier won't want to miss this call."

"One moment," the woman said, and George found himself listening to the faint music again. Not his kind. George had a quiet collection of CDs, for him alone, torchy stuff, definitely off limits to his mother, stuff to paint by, Dinah Washington, Linda Ronstadt, Liza Minnelli. Some things just don't . . .

"Yes," came a voice over the phone almost whispering.

"It's me," George said, his voice still disguised. "You asked me to call you at ten. I'm calling you."

"Who is this?"

"Burt Chambers from the Tool and Die," said George.

"I don't know what the hell . . ."

"Look, Mr. Dozier, I'm just doing what—"

"Dozier?"

"Are you Carl Dozier?" asked George.

"Harvey Rozier," the man said with exasperation that George thought was fully justified.

"Look," said George. "Is this or isn't this three-one-two-one-one-one-one?"

"No," said Rozier, looking at the number on the phone. "It is not."

"I'm sorry," George said with a sigh. "I'm having a bad day."

Rozier hung up. So did George.

He had watched the Rozier house for three weeks. Every night. Looking for a house in Saginaw Park with signs of money, a wall or tall trees, and no dogs. The Rozier house, a red brick that looked a little like a castle, stood at the end of a cul-de-sac and down a drive. George had had his handyman card ready when he approached the house the first time, right after the mailman left. George had been ready to whip the card out in case he had overlooked a maid, a pool man, a relative. He'd driven right to the front door and rung the bell. No answer, but George was just setting up, taking no chances. Nice place. Big. He went for the mail, found out he was at the home of Harvey and Dana Rozier.

George returned to the street every few days and nights but never to the cul-de-sac. It wasn't the only house he checked out. He had six others on the line in suburbs as far

4

north as Highland Park and as far south as Morgan Park. It was part of the job. He found Rozier's name and office number in the Chicago White Pages—Harvey N. Rozier, Investment Consultant. The home phone was unlisted. No big problem to go to Rozier's office on LaSalle Street near City Hall, find out what kind of car the man had, and get a look at him. Rozier was a big man, maybe George's age, probably a little younger. Good looking. Worked out. Serious guy with a fake smile. Losing his hair and combing it forward. Good clothes.

Two days after first seeing Rozier, George saw Dana Rozier. Harvey had a tasteful '94 Lexus. She had a red Mazda sports car. From a distance she looked younger than her husband. Up close, when he checked her out when she went out shopping, she looked tight, blond, maybe a little too skinny, at least for George's taste, but sending out signals of money. Just the jewelry she wore for an afternoon out would have been enough to keep George in food, rent, paint, and nights in the local bars for half a year, even if he got only a nickel on the dollar.

The Roziers had no kids and no live-in maid. A couple of black women—looked like mother and daughter—came to the house Mondays, Wednesdays, and Fridays. Stayed all day. Left at five on the dot. Had their own key. George was sure they'd be the number-one suspects the night he cleaned the place out.

One night when he was watching the Roziers, a Tuesday, Harvey came out to the Lincoln dressed like Fred Astaire and his wife like Ginger. Tux, gown, the works. George followed them downtown, where they let a valet park them in front of the Bismarck. George considered making it back to their house in Saginaw and doing it fast, but he had learned to be careful. Two times downtime for felony made a thief careful. Maybe they were just picking someone up, having a few drinks, and then having a party at home. Maybe a hell of a lot of things. George wasn't the valet parking kind, but he didn't want to lose the Roziers.

He pulled into a loading zone and jumped out as the couple moved slowly into the hotel. It would probably mean a ticket, but it might not if he was fast. A ticket might make George think twice. What if he became a suspect and they found he had been parked in front of the hotel where the burglary victims were on the same night? What if? What if? What if? If he had a ticket when he came out, George would cross off the Rozier house.

George wasn't dressed for a downtown hotel but he didn't look bad either. He was shaved, wore black denim slacks and a button-down pale gray shirt with a low-key black leather zippered jacket.

The lobby was full of men in tuxes and women with gowns and jewels whose addresses George would have loved to have.

George asked a kid bellhop what was going on.

"Chamber series," he said.

"Music?"

"I guess," said the kid, looking impatient.

"You said series?"

"Every Tuesday this month, next month. There's a program in front of the door," the kid said. "All I know."

George had checked. A black-and-white photograph of a Chinese or Korean or something girl with long hair and a cello between her legs was stuck to the tripod in front of the door through which couples were hurrying.

They were being nodded in by a tall, no-nonsense woman in her fifties whose black-with-white streaked hair was pulled back tight and topped by a tiara worth no more than a few hundred dollars, tops.

"Single tickets?" George had asked innocently.

"Series only," the woman said, nodding more people in, though most of them didn't pause for her approval.

George nodded and checked the schedule on the tripod. There were none being distributed.

It was perfect. Every Tuesday. No holidays in the way. Concert went from eight to eleven. George didn't have a ticket when he went out to his car.

It looked perfect. Still, George was taking no chances. He was in the lobby of the Bismarck the following week. The Roziers showed up just before eight with another couple, older, maybe in their sixties, dignified. The man was tall, neatly trimmed white hair and mustache, and the woman a little on the thin side but good looking for her age. For most pros this would have been enough, but not for George. He checked them on the following Tuesday. The Roziers and the old couple were there, and George noted that the woman with the tight hair greeted them by name. He stayed far from the door so she didn't see him, but he could hear her confident voice syruping across the lobby. Someone called her Mrs. Gabriel. It was enough.

Time. George tore up the scrap of paper with the number of the Bismarck concert room phone and flushed it down the toilet. His mother had turned off the television more than two hours earlier and had screamed down to George that she was going to sleep and if he got hungry there was a noodle pudding in the fridge he could stick in the microwave.

George looked around his room, checked his watch. Blanket rolled down on the bed, paintings stacked against the walls, green chair that had been his father's near the window, battered dresser needing glue for loose drawers. Not much, but it beat a cell.

George didn't hide his tools anymore and he didn't use traditional burglary gear. He carried everything in a padded toolbox, only things a decent mechanic, plumber, or handyman might carry: tubing cutter, glass cutter, and minicutter, rib-joint pliers, adjustable-end wrench, a pair of screwdrivers, an Allen wrench, a close-quarters hacksaw, a curved-claw hammer, a wood chisel, a utility knife, and a rasp. Handyman. That was his cover. Hard to shake, even with the two neatly folded linen laundry bags at the bottom of the toolbox. Ex-con trying to make it as handyman, claiming that all of his work was small and for cash if he got caught. Always an angle. Call a guy down the street from where you were breaking. Ask if you could come over and give him a no-obligation estimate on fixing his front steps or loose-shingled roof. Bluebots pick you up and you claim you're at the wrong house. Walked right in after you knocked. The door was open. Way beyond suspicious but hard to prove, even if they nailed you inside, providing you weren't carrying goods. Criminal trespass was the worst he figured he could get.

He looked in the bathroom mirror.

Thin guy in the mirror looked OK. Clean shaven, jaw a little weak, blue-gray eyes, clean but not-so-even teeth, a full head of brown-gray hair. Work clothes. Not black, to blend in and wind up looking suspicious, but faded jeans, red-and-black flannel shirt. Shoes, three-year-old faded Rockports. Sneakers might make someone suspicious.

Checked the watch again, not one he'd stolen. One he had paid twenty-five bucks and change for, about what your not-successful ex-con handyman trying to make a living might wear.

Satisfied, George picked up his toolbox and saw something on the canvas resting on the easel near the window. The left eye of the woman at the bar was too large. He would have to correct that or at least check to see if the morning light gave him a better perspective. George went out the door and into the cool spring night. He had a private entrance to his mother's house. After George's father had died, Wanda Eupatniaks had married her husband's best friend, Laslo Skutnik, a widower with a pension from the slaughterhouse, a Swift and Company employee for almost forty years. Wanda and Laslo had vegetated together in front of the television till Laslo died a year and a day after George's father, leaving Wanda a new name and a comfortable, mortgage-paid house.

When he first got out, George had rented a small apartment in the house of the Vivlachkis, a few blocks away off of Diversey. The Vivlachkis were a nice old couple who knew George's mother. They called him Gregor. They went to sleep early and didn't hear too well. They liked Gregor. He painted a portrait of their dead son, Stanley, from an old photograph. It hung over the mantelpiece right next to Jesus Christ Almighty his own self. But money had gotten a little tight. A few jobs had to be canceled. Too many risks. And old man Vivlachki started to get too curious about George's sources of income and late nights out. It was easier to move in with his mother, who couldn't make it down the stairs to his rooms and who watched television most of the day, went to bed early, slept like a mountain, and snored like a volcano.

George shivered with the chill. Couldn't have been more than forty-five degrees. Fine for a Chicago spring. Sky dark, looking like it couldn't make up its mind to piss or snow. If the temperature dropped and it snowed while he was on the way to the job, George would turn around and go home or maybe head for Unikle's bar, maybe get lucky and run into Mary Ann Zdrubecki, whose husband, Cinch, was doing four short ones for holding up a 7-Eleven.

Snow was too many chances. Rain had its problems too, but rain kept people off the streets where they might remember seeing a man with a toolbox.

Among the skills George had picked up was bringing the dead back to life. Dead cars. Both of his brothers were mechanics, Ernie at a Volvo dealer on Elston, Sandor with his own gas station up north on Howard Street. Before he retired with emphysema, George's father had been a mechanic for a series of Brunswick bowling alleys owned by Davey Moran, who was just as big a Litvak as any Eupatniaks but knew which side his alley was buttered on.

George's car was a Toyota Corolla, dark green, three years old. Nothing suspicious on the outside, but it ran almost as silent as a submarine. Part of the job. Keep your tools clean and silent. The Toyota was a tool. Tools don't work and you take an extra chance.

Toolbox sat on the seat next to him. Right in the open. Windows closed on a cool night. Radio playing some talk show guy saying it was fine to look at women's asses and think about how they'd move. Guy was right. Natural to look and think. Can't stop looking and thinking.

He drove past a series of bombed-out two-stories with hot dog, fried fish, or auto parts on the street level. Apartment or two above. Woman over Wynette's Fried Shrimp in the window. Skinny. A shadow, hugging herself. Fear? Cold? What? And he was gone, almost bumper-to-bumper with a dirty white van. He'd paint that scene when he finished the painting he was working on, the one of the lonely woman at the bar. He could see the woman over Wynette's, little more than a shadow, the night lights of the fish house below her casting yellow on the street. He wanted to capture the smell of the place and the lonely sag of her thin body.

And the guy on the radio with a raspy voice said, "How about breasts?" George didn't like music. He liked voices, people talking, keeping him company. He didn't have to talk to them. They told the news or talked in cycle two, nonstop, nervous talk, saying nothing. In the Patniks analysis, developed during his years in the joint, cycle one was fear coming out as anger or depression. That could last anywhere from a month to a year. Cons seemed to vary their cycles depending on the length of their sentences. A murder one could be angry for years. Cycle three was the most dangerous and looked the least like trouble. In cycle three the con gets mellow, shows no emotion, looks as if his mind is off somewhere listening to Sade. There's a space around these cons. It's the place they've found a troubled peace. Break in on it and they've got no place to retreat and nothing much to lose. Cycles one and two you see coming. Cycle threes . . .

The hard gray and dusty red of squat city buildings gave way to hulking factories and then the expressway. Concrete and green exit signs. Cars with drivers minding their own business. The sound of swishing tires and radio voices.

George got off at Peterson, turned onto Lincoln, and drove past hot dog stands, one-fuck motels, and Jew bookstores. A Buick dealer and a barbecue restaurant on his left, Goodyear tire center on his right, and then Devon. Different world. Trees, houses with space between them even on the main drag, too cold for people to be walking or meeting with their neighbors over the fence.

When he got to the Roziers' street, George checked for dog walkers. Unpredictable. Always a problem. Dog walkers. Who could predict the bladder control of a poodle? George knew of two burglars personally who had been

10

turned up because of dog walkers with notebooks or good memories.

He pulled into the driveway of the Rozier house at the end of the cul-de-sac. He drove over the neatly fitted red bricks and sat for a few seconds looking at the lights in the house. He was sure the Roziers had left the lights on to discourage people like George Patniks. They had left the lights on every week when they went to the chamber music series.

"In for it all now, George," he said to himself, as he had said before every job he had done in the last two decades. He stepped out of his car.

He hurried around the side of the house to the kitchen. George could hear music inside the house. He didn't stop. He knew the radio was on a timer, that the station would change every fifteen or twenty minutes as if someone were fooling with the dials.

The dining room window at the side of the house was wired as he remembered and expected. It wasn't a bad system, connected to both the local police and the Everwatch System office. George put down the toolbox, took the glass cutter from his pocket, checked the second hand on his watch, took a breath, and moved quickly to cut a more or less round hole in the glass. From the moment he began the cut, George knew he had to hurry. Everwatch Security gave the homeowner a full twenty-five seconds to get to the phone and turn off the system. He reached in and opened the window and climbed in. The music was loud, something classical, light, breaking champagne glasses and giggles that were implied rather than released. He hurried through the dining room with its eight high-backed wooden chairs around a table with spindly animal legs and went right through the kitchen door, heading for the phone on the wall near the back door. He put the tool chest down, opened it almost silently, and pulled out the wire cutter. He pulled the phone from the hook on the wall, turned it over, found the wires he was looking for, and snipped neatly. He was breathing hard as he checked his watch. Sixteen seconds.

George had made it with nine seconds to spare.

A sound from above, like footsteps. Somebody home? A creaking step or floorboard? Hard to tell over the blaring music. George stood for twenty seconds or so until he was reasonably satisfied that no one was there. He hurried across the kitchen floor.

George needed no flashlight. The Roziers had provided him with all the light he needed and more than he wanted. He planned to move fast, check the case spots, go for the jewelry, and forget the big things. If he was lucky, the Roziers would come home, maybe have a drink, and head for bed without noticing the small hole in the window and not discovering that the kitchen phone was out of order at least till the next morning.

George had his hand on the kitchen door when his world exploded.

Voices. From beyond the door. Two. Arguing. Sounded like a man and woman. Coming downstairs. Coming fast.

Shit. Shit. Shit. Shit. Go for the window. Too late. Too far. They were heading for the kitchen. Fast. The kitchen was big. One night-light near the sink. Table, modern, and six chairs around it to his left. Working table in the middle of the room. Big butcher's block. Walls lined with cupboards, dishwasher, refrigerator. Door. A pantry or closet. George stepped inside.

Pantry. No window. The toolbox. His toolbox. It was out there, sitting in the middle of the kitchen. Well, maybe not the middle, but still hard to miss. Too late. The kitchen door was opening. George closed the pantry door, praying that it was well oiled and that the toolbox would be overlooked.

The kitchen door burst open.

"Harvey, Harvey," the woman wept as George pressed his back against a shelf of cans. "Please."

Harvey didn't answer. And the woman sounded weird.

What were they doing home? What the hell were they . . . ?

Something scratched across the tile floor.

"God, no. Please."

George moved from the wall of cans and pitty-pittied to the pantry door, opening it a crack. Pitty-pitty on frightened little cat Rockports.

The white nightgown of Dana Rozier was bright with blood and open to her stomach. She staggered backward toward the kitchen door. Harvey Rozier strode silently toward her. He wore some kind of white floor-length smock that made him look like a mad scientist George had seen in some English horror movie about zombies on channel 32.

Dana Rozier was going for the door. She had no chance of making it without help, and George was sure that if he stepped out of the pantry he'd be covered in his own blood within a couple of heartbeats. Rozier was too big for him, in better shape, and carrying the biggest fucking knife George Patniks had ever seen.

George pushed the door open a little more, wondering what the hell Rozier was planning to do. That was when Rozier tripped over George's toolbox. The knife flew out of his hand and spun across the floor. Rozier went sprawling, smock billowing awkwardly.

Dana Rozier went for the door, losing strength. Too many bolts. She reached for the phone as her husband got to his knees and scrambled for the bloody knife.

"No, no, no," Dana Rozier panted, unwilling, unable to turn her back on her husband.

George, standing in the pantry doorway, watched her hit three numbers, 911 for sure. But she heard nothing as Rozier found the knife. There was nothing she could hear because George had cut the phone wires.

Too late. Too late now. Rozier was on top of her, pulling his wife from the phone, plunging the knife in wherever her flailing arms let him through. Face, eye, scalp, chest, arms. She crumpled, whimpering, and Rozier went on.

George didn't move, couldn't move. Rozier knelt over what was left of his dying wife, panting, his white smock splotched like a bloody Rorschach.

George watched the exhausted man's face and heaving body and knew what was about to happen. Rozier looked back across the room to see what had tripped him. His eyes found the toolbox. He panted heavily, not understanding, and his eyes moved across the room, finding George almost instantly.

Their eyes met. Rozier puzzled, weary, confused. George Patniks in panic. Rozier tried to rise, using the knife to prop himself up like an old man with a cane.

George's legs were trembling and nausea tickled inside his stomach and went for his throat. A sound came from George and he knew he was running, his feet sliding on the tile floor, knowing that if he went down, Rozier's knife would get him, that the dead woman's blood would snare and bind him. His back was turned to Rozier now, and he had no idea how close the man might be. George sucked in air and ran for the window through which he had cut the hole. He tucked his head between his arms and threw his body against glass and wood, hoping it would shatter, but it didn't, not completely. He tumbled into cool air, rolling on his back, arm cut. He caught a glimpse of Rozier's shadow at the window, a ghostly, sheeted shadow carrying a bloody knife, panting.

George got to his feet and ran, ran for his car, forgetting about cuts, slashes, and murder, forgetting his tool case, and ignoring the certainty that he had fouled his underwear and legs.

He slid into the driver's seat of the Toyota, cracking his knee against the steering wheel, and locked the door with one hand as he turned the key with the other. Rozier wasn't at the door. Not yet. He threw the car in reverse and tried to keep calm, keep from hitting the birdbath or the bushes and slamming into the trees that lined the driveway.

He let his eyes move upward quickly as he screeched backward into the night, and what he saw was as frightening as the murder he had witnessed.

Rozier hadn't moved from the window. He stood, motionless, looking directly at George Patniks. Their eyes met again as George hit the gas and swirled madly and loudly down the red-brick driveway. George wouldn't swear, but he was pretty goddamn sure that Harvey Rozier was smiling at him.

In Which Things Go Awry

Pitty-Pitty Patniks was wrong. Harvey Rozier had not been smiling. His evening had gone even worse than the burglar's. When he was sure that the madly retreating car of the burglar hadn't struck a tree, a house, or a pedestrian, Harvey turned back into the room, wiped the handle of the knife on his linen floor-length robe, and threw it in the general direction of his wife's body. He didn't want to look at her. It had taken months of fear and anger to go through with the murder, and now he wanted to, had to, convince himself, hypnotize himself as best he could into believing, that the lie he would tell was truth.

Harvey had seen many of his clients lie so convincingly to the press and the Internal Revenue Service that he was sure they had convinced themselves of the lie. Trudeau. Martin Trudeau, millionaire leader of the Evangelical Free Church of Christ, had lied to the IRS. Took a lie detector test. Results were inconclusive. Could Harvey pass a lie detector test? Possibly, he thought, forcing himself to look at Dana's body once more to be sure she was dead. Possibly.

One thing to plan. Harvey was a great planner. Another thing to execute. He hadn't planned on Dana running down the stairs. He wanted it to look as if she had been surprised in bed by an intruder. Now he had a trail of blood, bloody footprints, and a goddamn witness.

She was dead.

He tried not to think about the burglar, at least not consciously at first. He had a plan. He had to execute the plan. He would . . . He had stripped naked except for the sneakers. He washed his bloody, surgically gloved hands, dried them on a relatively clean corner of the robe, and got a plastic Hefty garbage bag from under the sink. He threw in the white linen robe he'd purchased two weeks ago on a business trip to Lexington and carried the bag to the back door, taking care that it picked up no blood. He opened the door, stepped out, and walked to the brick driveway, where he removed the sneakers and surgical gloves and dropped them into the plastic garbage bag. There was a faint trail of partially footprinted blood leading from the house.

If the burglar goes to the police, Harvey thought, hurrying barefoot up the stairs, he runs the risk of being accused of Dana's murder, but this guy was a burglar, not a murderer. Harvey got in the shower and turned on the hot water, letting it scald his chest. He covered himself with soap—liquid soap—head to toe. Had to be fast. Harvey was shivering, trembling. He heard something and threw open the shower curtains. Had some neighbor heard the damn burglar go through the dining room window and called the police? Nothing, no one, just the blare of music from the stereo speaker downstairs. He closed the curtains but not all the way, pushing back the fantasy of Dana as a blood-drenched zombie coming up the stairs with a knife in her stained hand.

And the burglar, the burglar, goddamn it, the burglar. The burglar might not be very bright. He might not think it through, might not realize that he was in big trouble if he stepped forward. He might go to the police and describe what he had seen, identify Harvey as Dana's killer. Would he be believed? Would he reemerge when he had calmed down in a week, two, a month, and try to blackmail him?

Harvey turned off the water and stepped out of the shower, reaching for a towel.

Had to hurry. Think on the way.

He was back in his tux and down the stairs, avoiding the trail of Dana's blood on the carpet. One last quick look around. The door to the kitchen was closed.

"All right," he said aloud, and the sound of his own voice made his hands tremble. "All right," he demanded, and his hands obeyed. "What have I forgotten? The tool-box."

He moved back to the kitchen door, opened it with his elbow, avoiding the bloody trail, and went straight to the burglar's toolbox. He wiped the box with a dish towel and left it sitting in the middle of the room for an instant, an island in a sea of blood. Then he picked up the toolbox, holding it away from his body, went to the sink, washed off the already-drying blood, and moved to the door to the garage, glancing at Dana's deep-red-against-white corpse. She had stopped bleeding. He hid the toolbox in plain sight, beginning to panic, already making up an excuse—loose bowels, nausea—if the concert was over when he got back to the Bismarck. He checked himself for blood stains and found none.

By the time he returned with the Franklins to discover Dana's body, the doorknob would be a blur of finger and palm prints.

It was the best he could do. It wasn't quite the way he had planned, but . . .

He went out the side door and walked barefoot to the head of the driveway. Behind the house, through the trees at the end of the cul-de-sac, Harvey made his way carefully along the narrow path. Not much light, but enough. A thin spring rain tapped against the trees, which were just starting to get a new coat of green leaves, black in the moonless and starless night. He was a dark Santa carrying a dark bag of blood. No one in sight on Kilgore, the next street south, where he had parked the rented Geo Prizm. He opened the trunk, threw in the bag, closed the trunk quietly, and got into the driver's seat, where he closed the door just hard enough to turn off the "door ajar" light. He put on the socks and shoes he had left on the passenger seat and drove away slowly, watching the dark houses on either side of the street, listening to the rain start to beat harder on the roof.

It wasn't till he hit Howard Street and was heading for the expressway that he slammed the door firmly.

Check the time. A little over an hour since he had left the men's room at the Bismarck and walked quickly to the Geo in the Grant Park underground lot. He was way off, but he still had more than an hour, even if the quartet were incompetent and rushed through the Mozart and the Vivaldi.

He pulled the baseball cap over his eyes and drove, Kennedy to Eisenhower, back into the Grant Park underground lot, careful not to break the speed limit. The night attendant didn't even glance at him.

Still twenty minutes. Should make it easily.

Park in a corner. Car door echoing. Car trunk echoing. No one in sight. No sound of approaching cars. Lot not full but not empty for this hour. He would wait a few days, maybe a week, pick up the car, and return it to Hertz.

Harvey took the garbage bag in his arms and hurried to the garbage can near the escalator. No footsteps behind or in front. Nothing moving in the shadows of the concrete pillars. He shoved the bag into the garbage can and heaped empty bottles and stale food-covered McDonald's bags over it.

Time left. Time left.

He moved quickly but didn't run up the escalator and onto the street. The hotel was half a block away. Raining harder. He couldn't go back wet. He ran down the escalator, which fought him with each step, and searched frantically for something to cover himself with. A cardboard box lay limp behind the garbage can in which he had hidden the plastic bag. He grabbed the carton, ran to the street, shielded himself as the wind off the lake tried to tear his cover from his hands. Down the alley behind the hotel, he found the service entrance door he had propped open. It was still open. He dropped the soggy brown carton and went up the stairs, shoes resounding, the smell of something stale and sweet in the air.

He opened the door carefully and struggled to catch his breath. No one in sight to his left. Down the corridor two old men in tuxedos who had ducked out on the concert stood smoking. He pulled out his comb, used it, and decided he couldn't wait to fully control his breath.

Harvey eased out of the stairwell and into the men's room. Empty. He washed his hands, looked at himself in the mirror, brushed back his wisps of hair, splashed his face with cold water, and stepped into the hall near the performance room. Empty except for the two men smoking and whispering, not looking his way.

Harvey slipped into the concert room. Rows of backs were to him. No one seemed to turn. On the raised platform before the several hundred people on cushioned folding chairs, a thin, young Oriental woman attacked a violin, eyes closed to show her intensity and commitment. Harvey eased into the chair he had moved to the rear of the room. Ken and Betty Franklin were in the second row, wedged in.

Harvey picked up the small tape recorder from the floor under the chair, clicked it off, and dropped it into his pocket. He would listen to the tape as soon as he could, listen for anything unusual, a slight mistake or miscue, a coughing fit, something he could refer to, to prove he had sat through the performance.

The instruments came to a shrill decision to end. Applause. He had made it back with more than twenty minutes to spare. The two old men who had been smoking in the corridor came in and stood, joining the applause and the bows of the performers.

People filed past Harvey, talking of where they were going to get coffee or a drink, making soft patter about the performance.

The Franklins found him. They were older than the Roziers by almost twenty years, a pair of surrogate parents and much more. She a handsome society joiner. He the senior partner of the law firm of Kyle, Timkin, and O'Doul, with offices on the same floor as Harvey's in the John Hancock Building. Harvey had left his Lexus in the garage "in case Dana might need it" and had reluctantly agreed to go with the Franklins and let Ken drive. This was shortly after Dana had become nauseated just before they were scheduled to leave. Nothing terrible, but nothing pleasant either.

Touch of the flu. It was going around. People had even been hospitalized.

When the Franklins had arrived, Harvey insisted on staying home. Dana insisted that he go and have a good time. The Franklins promised to bring him right home after the concert.

"Did you call Dana?" Betty asked.

"No," said Harvey.

"Perhaps you should . . ." Betty continued.

"I don't want to wake her if she's managed to get to sleep."

"Let's just get you back home and see how she's doing," said Ken.

Harvey let himself be driven, forced himself to engage in small talk about brunch on Sunday and whether they should try to get a box together for the opera season. The Lyric was doing two Verdis. Dana loved Verdi.

Thirty minutes after they left the Bismarck, they stepped out of the Franklins' Lincoln and saw the broken dining room window and bloody footprints in the driveway.

Harvey ran to the door. Unlocked. He opened it and ran in, being sure that Ken was right behind him and Betty a few steps behind, bleating like a goat.

Harvey started for the stairway.

"This way," Ken shouted and led the way along the trail of blood to the kitchen.

The long night had just begun for Harvey Rozier.

Doctors

The doctor did not like Chicago.

The doctor, who had been in the city for almost four months now, thought that Chicago was a very dangerous place. Certainly much more dangerous than East Lansing, Michigan, where he had spent almost two years treating and being exposed to AIDS patients.

His name was Berry, Jacob Berry. He was thin, nervous, and wore a starched blue lab shirt with his last name stitched in an even darker blue on the pocket just to the left of his heart. Dr. Berry's principal source of income was giving annual physicals to Chicago Police Department officers and personnel, a noncontract deal Jacob's brother had wrangled through a political connection in the Cook County Democratic party.

Jacob turned to the policeman in the chair, hoping he was giving off the aura of an experienced, calm, and all-knowing physician. It was difficult with these policemen and women, nothing like the dead-eyed men and women at the AIDS clinic in East Lansing from which he had escaped 122 days ago. He counted the days but he was about to give up counting. East Lansing and the AIDS clinic were not as frightening as Chicago.

"You hate it in Lansing. So come to Chicago," his brother, also a Dr. Berry, had urged.

"Isaac," he answered. "I have no hospital affiliation, no patient history, very little saved, a ..."

"I'll find you something," Isaac Berry said to his younger brother. "A deal here. Nice and simple. I find you something, let you know, and you can say yes or no. Can it hurt?"

"No," he answered, intrigued by the possibility of escape from the faces of endless agony. Until Isaac's call he had not admitted how depressed he had become at the AIDS clinic. When Isaac, as good as his word, called back in less than three weeks with a fully equipped suite in Uptown he could rent at a very reasonable rate and the guarantee of an average of twenty-five full physicals and other referrals from the Chicago Police Department, Jacob took it. He had no idea what Uptown was. Now he was finding out.

The Uptown suite had three rooms, all small. The waiting room had five chairs covered in faded orange Naugahyde, a small book rack containing nothing, white walls that needed painting, and two reproductions of paintings by van Gogh, both of flowers. The reception desk was enclosed with a sliding glass door. Jacob Berry had not yet hired a receptionist and the prospect of having a nurse to help him was well into the future. The office/examining room held an old wooden desk with a wooden swivel chair behind it, a row of wooden book racks containing his small supply of the thick and the deadly, an examining table with two chairs, a tiny sink in a corner that was very stingy with hot water, and a white metal cabinet containing a minimum of samples from the drug company detail men who had welcomed him to his new practice. It didn't seem like much.

But the men had come. Policemen of all sizes and ages and problems, ranging from near exhaustion to failing eyesight, cancer, and long-abused organs. There were those who had bodybuilder torsos and those, like the one he had to talk to now, who looked like a good breeze would carry them out to Lake Michigan.

Their eyes were the same. A moist knowing. They looked around slowly, usually without moving their heads. And then when you spoke to them, their eyes met yours and held. The cops in general made Dr. Berry uncomfortable, but a lot less uncomfortable than the patients in East Lansing. It was the city that had gotten to Jacob almost from the minute he arrived. Dark shadows, insane headlines, sullen and frightened people walking the streets, cursing each other, making offers.

The policeman's name was Abraham Lieberman. He was almost dressed. He glanced toward the window as an el train screeched into the Argyle Station going south. The noise wasn't deafening, but since the platform was only fifteen feet from the window, its arrival gave pause to the conversation and reminded Dr. Berry of why his rent was so low. The rapid deterioration of the neighborhood, the Vietnamese gang extortionists, the el train almost within touching distance had certainly sent the previous occupant fleeing to the suburbs.

"Well," Dr. Berry tried again, looking at the clipboard containing lab results and notes and trying to strike a relaxed pose as he leaned against the sink and adjusted his glasses. "I've got the results of your lab tests here and—" And he suddenly remembered. His pink face went white.

"Doctor," said Lieberman, "are you all right?"

"I . . . yes," Dr. Berry said as the train pulled away.

Two days earlier Dr. Berry had made the mistake of opening the blinds to let in some natural light. He had been carrying a syringe filled with a flu injection for the policewoman sitting on the examining table. A train had pulled in next to his window and a trio of young men, dark and grinning, had been looking at him. One of the young men, no more than seventeen or eighteen, wearing a backward baseball cap, had produced a knife, which he pointed at Dr. Berry. The one with the knife urged the others to get off the train. The one with the baseball cap had shouted something at Dr. Berry that sounded through the windows and the rumble of the train as it began to move. "I'm bean bag," he had said, pointing to himself and at Dr. Berry, who had stood rigid, unable to turn away.

The boys had laughed.

Now, with the policeman in front of him, Dr. Berry suddenly knew what the boy had mouthed.

"I'll be back," Dr. Berry whispered.

"You have to leave?" Lieberman said as he finished tying his shoes.

"No," said Dr. Berry.

Dr. Berry tried to pull himself back from memory and looked into the sad, steady eyes of Abraham Lieberman. The hangers-on, the Alter Cockers, at the T & L Deli on Devon Avenue, which Abe's brother, Maish, owned, were evenly divided as to whether Abe looked more like a slightly dyspeptic dachshund or an underweight bloodhound. Lieberman, it could not be denied, was not an imposing figure at five seven and hovering around 145 pounds. He looked a good five years older than his sixty-two years. His brother, Maish, definitely a well-fed beagle, thought Lieberman looked like an undernourished Harry James. Maish's fruitless efforts to "put some meat on" his brother had begun almost half a century earlier, and though Abe had been a willing consumer, he had remained thin and in need of tolerant suspenders.

"It's not the amount, not even the quality," Maish had said with a resigned sigh. "It's your metabolism, Abe. You burn up straight-fat corned beef before it has time to get into your system."

Lieberman's wife, Bess, thought her husband, with his curly gray hair and little white mustache, looked like a distinguished lawyer or doctor.

But each morning when Abe looked into his mirror, usually after an almost sleepless night, he saw only the face of his father. The man in the mirror had a little more hair, maybe a fuller mouth, but it was the same face.

"Here," said Lieberman, stepping over to Dr. Berry and guiding him to the chair. "Sit."

Dr. Berry, trying to come out of his daze, let himself be led and sat. He clung to the clipboard and file and hugged them to his chest.

"A cup of water?" Lieberman said softly.

Dr. Berry nodded and Lieberman moved across the room for a small Dixie cup. He took the cup to the sink. The cold water was tepid. He filled the cup, crossed the room, and handed it to Dr. Berry, who loosened his grip on the clipboard and took the cup from Lieberman.

"Better?" Lieberman asked.

Dr. Berry nodded.

"It's my brother's fault, Isaac," Dr. Berry explained.

Dr. Berry, his temples touched with premature gray that matched his eyes, a full, dark mustache above his lip, looked to Lieberman like either a young man trying to look older or an older man trying to look younger.

"What's your first name?" Lieberman said, moving across the room to rest against the desk.

"My . . . ?"

"It's not Barry?" Lieberman asked. "Barry Berry?"

"No."

"Good," said Lieberman, folding his arms.

"My name is Jacob."

"You're Jewish?"

"Yes."

"Married?"

"No more."

"Gay?"

"No."

Lieberman shook his head. He would pass this information on to Bess, who was looking for a suitable professional replacement for their daughter Lisa's husband. Lisa had walked out on Todd Cresswell with Lieberman's two grandchildren. She had declared her independence, ten years after it was fashionable to do so, and moved in with Abe and Bess.

"I'm fine now," said Dr. Berry.

"You want to tell me?" asked Lieberman.

Somewhere on the street two stories below them an argument started in an Asian tongue. The arguers moved away as Dr. Berry took a deep breath and told about the three young men on the el train.

"You have a gun?" Lieberman asked.

"A gun?"

"Here, in the office, a gun."

"No."

25

"Consider it," said Lieberman. "Five years ago I'd have said no, but today . . ."

"You think those three will really come back here?" Berry said, a quiver of fear in his voice.

"No," said Lieberman. "You want odds, I'd say ninety-eight to two they forgot you five minutes after the train left the station."

"Then . . . ?"

"You want to take a chance on two percent?" asked Lieberman. "And what about the ones who come looking for drugs?"

"I didn't need a gun in East Lansing," said Dr. Berry, adjusting his glasses.

"Sounds like one of the songs my grandson listens to," sighed Lieberman. "I didn't need a gun in East Lansing, but baby I could use one now."

The clipboard was wet now with perspiration from Berry's palms. He eased the board to his lap.

"I don't know how to get a gun, shoot one," he said softly.

"I'll tell you how to get one and where to go to learn to use it," said Lieberman. "This is a good neighborhood to have a gun in. Even if you haven't made faces with some fun-loving citizens."

"I'll think about it," said Berry, wiping his face with his sleeve. Much of the starch had gone out of the blue jacket.

"Good," said Lieberman. "I'll give you a call. Now . . ."

"Now?" said Berry.

"Now you tell me what, if anything, is wrong with me."

"Oh, yes."

Dr. Jacob Berry nodded, cleared his throat, made the effort, and looked down at the clipboard.

"Detective Lieberman—"

"Abe."

"Abe, your heart is fine. Your blood pressure is in check but I think you should stay on the Cardizem. You said you've had no migraines for almost six months?" He looked up at Lieberman, who still stood over him, arms crossed. Dr. Berry knew their positions should be reversed, but he wasn't ready to stand yet. He was familiar with blood, death, and violence from internship duty in Ann Arbor and his own practice in East Lansing, but that was violence and death to others and after the fact.

"No migraines," agreed Lieberman, checking his watch. "When I feel one coming I take a Fiorinal. Works."

"You . . . let me see," said Dr. Berry, running his finger down the sheet on the clipboard. "You still have elevated liver enzymes. You tested positive for hepatitis A, B, and C, but I understand—"

"I've had two biopsies," Lieberman recited. "Both negative. I've had this since I was a kid. Don't ask me why. Almost kept me off the force. Check on it. More than thirty years."

"Your liver is slightly enlarged."

"I'll make a note."

"Good," said Dr. Berry with a little more confidence and a sense that if he tried, he could stand. He remained seated. "I see no further significant deterioration of the knee joints. Any new pain? Different or . . . ?"

"No," said Lieberman.

"Arthritis can be—"

"Doc," Lieberman said.

"Yes."

"Is there a flashbulb, a snake with springs, something at the end of this box?" Lieberman said, checking his watch again.

"I'm not sure I . . ."

"I do this for a living, Jacob," Abe said. "You're the suspect who wants to confess and I should wait and let you dance around it till you're ready. But I'm the patient. You are the pro. And I have a vague but dwindling hope that I can make the Cubs game this afternoon."

"Your insomnia . . ." Dr. Berry tried.

"This sit-down isn't about insomnia, is it, Doc?"

Jacob Berry shook his head, pulled himself together, and stood.

"Do you drink? Your liver and—"

"Wine on the Sabbath. A beer maybe once a week, not even that."

"What do you eat? Normal day—yesterday?"

"Who remembers yesterday?" said Lieberman, his eyes firmly on the doctor's face. "I'll try. Coffee in the morning, with a toasted bagel, cream cheese, and lox. In the afternoon, let me see, a couple of hot dogs with the works and grilled onions. Another coffee. Dinner, that's easy. Bess made liver and onions. What's the problem, Jacob?"

Jacob Berry was looking more like a doctor now.

"You have a cholesterol level of almost three hundred. Your record says you have been warned twice and put on diets. You haven't paid attention to the diets, have you, Mr. Lieberman?"

"I watch, but a man—"

"We'll try a diet first. And this time we'll follow it to the letter."

"We? Your cholesterol level high too?"

"No."

"Then just say 'you will try a diet.' Humor me, please."

"When you've been on the diet for four months, we'll test again and decide if you need medication."

"Tell me about this diet, Jacob. Tell me quickly. I'm a good listener and I still harbor some small hope of getting to Wrigley Field this afternoon."

"We . . . you start by cutting all red meat. It would be best if you cut all fish and fowl, but let's see how you do without red meat. No alcohol. No milk or milk products. No butter."

"Hot dogs, corned beef, chopped liver . . . ?"

"Animal organs are definitely out."

"What," said Lieberman wearily, "do you think about assisted suicide?"

"What? I . . ."

"It's a joke, Jacob. I have too many responsibilities to die. My family would never forgive me. Anything else?"

"Your father and mother both died from heart-related problems," Dr. Berry said, consulting his clipboard.

"Yes. My father was eighty-six, my mother was eighty-one."

"I'd like you to see my brother, Isaac."

"Why? Does he have two heads?" Lieberman put up his hands. "Sorry, I have a useless hope that bad humor will sustain me through starvation."

"My brother is a cardiologist," Dr. Berry said in humorless confusion as Lieberman's beeper suddenly demanded attention.

The beeper went mad. Lieberman took the small black plastic box from his pocket and clicked it off.

"Use your phone?"

Dr. Berry nodded. Lieberman dialed the Clark Street Station, identified himself, and listened.

"He asked for me? . . . I don't remember. . . . Are you asking or telling? . . . Then I'm going. Give me the address. . . . Thank you. I'll meet you there. . . . I'm fine. How are you? . . . Good, then we're both fine. Good-bye."

Lieberman put down the phone and turned again to Dr. Berry.

"Give me your brother's number and address," said Lieberman, opening his notebook.

Jacob Berry had to get the address and information brochures on diet from his desk drawer. Lieberman took the stack, wrote down Dr. Isaac Berry's address and phone number, snapped his notebook shut, and put it in his pocket.

"How do you feel?" Jacob Berry asked.

"I'm breathing," said Lieberman, moving to the door, thinking that he probably looked a hell of a lot better than the frightened young man in front of him. "A good way to start any day."

With his hand on the door, Lieberman turned. He almost collided with Jacob Berry, who was following him.

"Couple more questions," Lieberman said. "You like music? Read?"

"Sure," said Berry, wondering where this was going.

"Classical—Mozart, Vivaldi?"

"Yes."

29

"Favorite authors?"

"I don't . . . I don't read much fiction."

Lieberman shrugged.

"Baseball. You like baseball?"

"Yes. I played at Evansville when I was an undergraduate."

Lieberman nodded.

"Position?"

"Second base," said Jacob.

Lieberman nodded as if this were essential information.

"I'll give you a call. We'll get you a gun, teach you how to use it. You get users in a neighborhood like this and they start thinking that doctors have a drug supply. You like brisket?"

"I haven't had any red meat in two years."

"You're healthy?"

"Yes."

"Turkey, chicken, duck?"

"Sure."

"Good."

Lieberman stepped through the door and across the small, empty waiting room.

"Detective Lieberman," Dr. Berry said.

"Abe."

"Abe, I feel confident that we can control your cholesterol. It could have been much worse. There are worse things."

Like coming home from a concert and finding your wife cut to pieces on the kitchen floor, Lieberman thought.

When the policeman was gone, Jacob felt a fingernail of fear along his spine. Lieberman had worn a pistol in the holster under his jacket. He took it off for the examination and Jacob glanced at it. The gun was frightening and fascinating. He would definitely feel better with one in his drawer, a gun he could pull out, show, feel protected by.

Jacob Berry took the four steps to the outer door and locked it. He had fallen into the habit of leaving his examining room door open and asking patients to identify themselves through the outer door before he let them in.

He went back to his office and pulled the blinds, sending the room from sun to fluorescent, shadowless light.

A Morning of Denial

George Patniks was upset. George Patniks was shaking. He had sketched out the scene without thinking. Sketched it in pencil directly onto the only piece of canvas he had stretched and ready—about three feet high and two feet wide. The kitchen, counters, phone, table, his own toolbox, and the figure of the man in the white robe standing over the fallen, pleading woman, who tried to protect herself with a thin arm.

He had removed the painting of the sad, smoking woman from his easel and placed it against the wall near his dresser.

He paused for a spark of time and looked at what he was doing. He had not sketched in the blood. Not yet. That would come later, when the color was right, when he felt it pulsing in his own veins.

But now he was nearly feverish. Above him his mother played the television, blaring, vibrating his ceiling like the top of a huge drum. Oprah, Donahue, Jenny Jones, Maury. George's mother was addicted and afflicted—addicted to television junk and afflicted with enormous diabetic legs.

Her furniture was fifty years old and the curlicue pattern was worn down to the hint of a memory from two generations of overweight Eupatniaks' bodies. George was an exception to the family rule. Maybe fat would suddenly spring on him when he wasn't prepared and he would wake up one morning looking like his mother, his Aunt Rosie, or his father until the cancer had chiseled him into a knotty stick, before it had taken him.

George's room was a mess, a clutter of paintings leaning

against one another on one wall—at least fifty paintings— paper on the floor, tubes of paint, capped but stained from previous bleedings of pigment, two palettes on the heavily and colorfully stained wooden table next to the easel near the window.

His bed, dresser, and a reasonably comfortable chair cramped themselves into a nook near the closet. He had his own bathroom with a toilet and shower. There were moments when it struck George that he had arranged and furnished his room so that it would look like a slightly larger version of his cell in Stateville.

But now, now he had a problem. He couldn't get the blue right. He mixed colors on his pallet with an ancient spoon. Whites, blues, even a little yellow, but he couldn't get the hue of the table and matching countertop in the Rozier kitchen. He had to find it. He couldn't compromise. He wiped hair from his eyes, sure that he was accidentally and incidentally painting himself like a movie Indian about to go to war against Custer.

His hands were blue now. He looked at the sketch of death on canvas and felt the as-yet-unfinished dead woman in the painting calling to him to get it right, telling him that he would be given no peace till he captured the scene in paint. It was worse than not remembering the tune of some song, the name of your first cell mate, the phone number of a woman you met at Unikle's Tap who wrote it down on something you stuck in your pocket and couldn't find.

"I'll get it. I'll get it. I'll get it," he muttered, competing with an angry, semiliterate skinhead on "Oprah" audible from above. George had known skinheads, pinheads, and Steelhead, heard them coughing and cursing, threatening and sobbing from nightmares in the cell block. He had heard them pitty-pat barefoot early in the morning like caged tigers at the Lincoln Park Zoo.

"Close," George said aloud. "Very close. Maybe."

He tried the blue he had mixed on the sketched tabletop. Decisions. Would it be just that little bit lighter on the canvas? Should the woman's eyes be open or closed? He had seen them both ways.

"All right," he sighed, clenching his fists in triumph. "That's the blue."

And he worked without knowing in words why. Ideas came and floated briefly, shimmering and flying away before he could examine them. Colors, shapes, and shadows demanded their place before him.

Maybe the painting would free him from the memory. He had offered a deal to whatever gods might be, but he was fast coming to the conclusion that there couldn't be any deals because there weren't any gods, though demons were a certainty. The deal had to be with the dead woman, a deal whereby the memory would be transferred from him to the canvas. Purged, clean. He would keep the painting, face to the wall, pay homage to it by looking at it from time to time, probably on a regular basis, same time each day or week. He could never sell it, probably never even show it to anyone.

"Can't keep you here," he said to the painting. "Not free, open, facing the fucking world. Can't show you. Can't sell you."

The memory of the woman pleading, dying, and him standing trapped, helpless inside the pantry had brought him awake four times in the short hours of the night before. He had fallen asleep quickly, easily as always, and slept lightly, as he had learned to do behind the walls and wire. George Patniks was not much of a dreamer, but last night . . .

The table was almost finished. He had slopped a bit over the lines that marked the edge of the table, but he would cover that when he painted the floor of the kitchen. The terrazzo floor would be a challenge. He wasn't quite sure of the pattern. He dug for it in his memory, begged, coaxed, and pleaded it forward. He looked at the rough sketch of the woman. She pleaded with him. No, she insisted.

George had seen violence, death, blood, and horror, but it had always been desperate or crazy men doing desperate and crazy things to one another with sharpened spoons, recreation yard stones, pipes unscrewed from the sink near the shoe shop. Throats cut, faces bashed. George had seen the pain of sodomy and the ecstasy of bleeding-nosed death from a crack overdose. A black guy named Corren who had raped a ten-year-old girl had his penis whacked off by another black guy named Zed-Zed who had a nine-year-old daughter on the outside. George had heard Corren scream, had seen him writhing, hands on the bloody stump, as two trustees hurried him on a stretcher down to the infirmary, holding the mutilated man away from the accompanying guard, who didn't want to get blood on his uniform. Those memories had passed and maybe this one would too, but he was sure it needed help, a lot of help.

Blue to the countertop.

"If that's what women want, I give it to 'em is all," a smug, insolent voice came from above, challenging Phil's, Oprah's, Bertice's, or Ricki's ready-for-battle and indignant audience.

He couldn't stand it, but he couldn't stop. He wanted to grab his jacket and run down to Unikle's, but the perfect blue had to go down on the canvas now. He would never be able to match it again. Fools and sinners laughed over his head. George knew that sound well. He painted thickly but in control and then and then and then the blue was down, finished, and George knew he was sweating through his floppy gray Mickey Mouse sweatshirt.

He wiped his brush on the stained chamois, rested it in the shell of thin turpentine, crossed the room, opened the door, and hurried up the narrow wooden steps.

When he hit the tiny kitchen, the voice of the insolent, shouting man was ricocheting off the walls. George stepped through the archway and moved past his mother, who sat half on her hip in her favorite chair. George turned the volume down on the TV and saw the face of a man who used to be a woman. Right under his face on the screen it said, "Kyle Anther, Used to Be a Woman." Kyle Anther was very young, crew cut, ring in one ear, tight jeans. He never did time, George thought, never saw, felt, or feared what should be feared.

"It was too loud?" his mother asked as George turned.

Wanda Eupatniaks Skutnik sat, a sad balloon of a woman

in a purple sack dress and faded purple slippers decorated with wilting purple satin flowers clinging to the toes. Wanda's dyed red hair was pulled back in a bun tied with a purple ribbon. She was color coordinated but it looked off. Her round face showed concern. Her eyes met her son's. She looked like a dish of blueberry ice cream with a cherry on top.

"It was a little too loud, Ma," he said. "Hard for me to . . . I'm painting."

She nodded.

"You look like a wild Indian," she said.

It was George's turn to nod.

Her son's painting, which did not please her, was the source of his income. Her son was a moderately successful artist. She told her sisters and brother, her other children, the few friends she still had, and the people at St. Agnes's Church that her son Gregor was a painter—not houses, but pictures people paid for.

"You hungry?" she asked.

"Don't know."

"I'll make you something," she said, starting to grunt herself out of the chair.

"No, Ma. I'll make you something."

But she was up and hobbling toward the kitchen. There was no stopping her, no point in argument. She would prepare scrambled eggs with onions and thick sausage. She had promised him this, a favorite.

"I'll turn the sound back up," he said, following her into the kitchen.

"Just a little," she said. "When we finish eating."

He sat, defeated, at the table, thinking about the white of the dead woman's nightgown, how he would capture the shadows and shade of that bloody gown. A commercial blared beyond the door and a woman with the voice of a young girl shouted a promise of forever clean teeth.

Onions, sausage frying. His mother cracking, stirring eggs and adding salt, salt she shouldn't eat. She selected a clove of garlic and shuffled for her garlic press.

"Take the television and the taste of my food and what do I have left?" she had asked more than once.

"No one's taking your television," George always said.

"You never know," his mother answered.

At the kitchen table, a small, square-topped collection of mismatched boards his grandfather and father had made, George folded his blue hands and tried to think.

Could the police find him? Maybe. Maybe not. There were no fingerprints on the toolbox or in the kitchen of the Roziers' house. But you didn't know anymore. It might not be fingerprints. They had machines, tests, gadgets, science.

Would they think he had killed the woman if they found him? Yes.

Would they believe what had happened when he told them? No.

And the murderer. George had seen his face and he had seen George's. Would he try to find George? Could he? George's name wasn't on the toolbox.

Wanda Skutnik hummed "Jezebel" softly as she worked, occasionally interrupting the hum with a few words she remembered.

"If ever a devil was born, without a pair of horns, hmm, hmm, hmmm, hmmm, hmmm. You know Frankie Laine is almost dead. Heart. I saw his picture. Is he a Negro?"

Maybe I should call Rozier, tell him I won't talk to the police, tell him I don't want anything, just to be left alone. I leave you alone and you live with what you did and you leave me alone and I live with what you did. Can't bring her back.

"He couldn't find me," George said.

"What? Gregor, you said? Frankie Laine couldn't find you?"

The frying pan sizzled and steamed.

"Nothing, Ma. Just something else."

He was hungry now. Garlic, onion, and sausage hungry. Two slabs of bread hungry. George would eat quickly and get back to the painting.

"Ma, how you feel about maybe going to visit Tommy?

57

You and me. We just pack, take off. Don't tell anyone where we're going."

Wanda turned completely around, ignoring the almost-finished meal simmering behind her.

"Gregor, you in trouble again?"

"No," he said, shaking his head. "There's a dealer in Seattle interested in my paintings. Could mean a lot of money."

Her wide deer eyes found his. He forced himself not to turn away.

"I'll ask Dr. Swoboda."

"We're not taking Dr. Swoboda," he said.

Wanda laughed.

"Get the plates and Coke," she said happily. "We can talk about it."

In Which a Door Closes

"He got somethin'. Scared we seen it. I tell you straight out. Seen it in his face. You did too. Tell me yes. Tell me no."

"You mean the ghost in the window?" Dalbert said.

"Straight out," Lonny said, shaking his head emphatically. "He's a fuckin' doctor. No lie. He's got somethin' worth somethin'."

"The white guy we seen from the el yesterday?" asked Iago. "In the blue shirt. Doctor or somethin'?"

"The same," said Lonny. "I showed him the blade and he shit nickels. No lie. You seen."

Dalbert shrugged, a what-the-hell-we've-got-nothing-better-to-do shrug.

Lonny Wayne, Albert "Dalbert" Davis, and Iago Simms sat in the Wayne apartment on Thirty-eighth. The view from the window was four square blocks of flattened rubble. Some said the city had leveled it to put in more public housing. Others said a trade or grade school was scheduled, but it looked more like a buffer zone between the ghetto and the hospital beyond. Lonny spent hours at the window fascinated by the emptiness, the children, and the garbage sifters turning over rocks and hoping for rats, sometimes even during the day. The Dysan brothers on six were all the time shooting rats from the window. Crazy mothers, Lonny thought, could kill someone. One rumor was that a new hospital was supposed to rise from the ashes, but Michael Reese Hospital was only a few blocks away. The four square blocks had been leveled more than three years ago.

"I say he got shit on toast is what I say," Iago said.

"An' me and Dalbert say we gonna take him and break him. He won't give us no trouble. Fuckin' A, all we gotta worry about is him havin' a fuckin' heart attack."

The apartment had two bedrooms, one for Lonny's mother and father, who were off working all the time in that damn suitcase factory for the damn Jews. The other bedroom was for Lonny's sister, but since Charletta was off at college in Urbana, Lonny had moved from the living room couch to Charletta's room, at least when she wasn't back on vacations.

The living room was big, the furniture old and heavy and ready to say, Sorry. No thanks. I've had enough of sagging and struggling under your feet and asses. I give up.

There was a photograph of Charletta and Lonny taken four years ago. Lonny hated it. The kid in the picture was all smiling teeth and no hair.

Lonny looked at the television. It was a Yogi Bear cartoon. The sound was turned off but Iago couldn't keep his eyes from the screen. Lonny turned to the window, looked out, and watched five little kids trekking over the rocks.

One day, last year, in the summer, a crazy old bum had built a little shack out of bricks and four rusted slabs of metal. The bum had made it through the first night, but on the second someone had kicked the place to shit and taken the bum's clothes and whatever else he had.

Charletta had been home for the summer, going to school at the U of I off the Dan Ryan, and Lonny had been sleeping on the couch with the window open. The bum's screaming woke him up. There wasn't much light to see by, but Lonny had seen two, maybe three figures running away and laughing. He would have swore one of them was Iago, but it was none of Lonny's business. He didn't even know Iago very well back then. The bum had danced around howling for what seemed like an hour. Lonny had closed the window and covered his head, but it hadn't done much good. Then the howling had stopped and Lonny was sure the bum was crying.

God, Lord Almighty, Lonny wished at the time and still

did that he had been one of those three or four figures in the night.

Rap sheet summaries:

Lonny Wayne, 18, six feet one, 190 pounds. African-American. Distinguishing characteristics: wide space between his top front teeth, pink knife scar on his right arm running from elbow to wrist, small dark scar shaped like a lightning bolt that runs through his right eyebrow. High school dropout. Arrests: sixteen, for crimes ranging from shoplifting, assault, and robbery to damage to a stolen vehicle. Convictions: none. Residence: mother's apartment.

Albert "Dalbert" Davis, 19, five feet eight, 202 pounds. African-American, Hispanic–Native American. Distinguishing characteristics: looks like a very dark Native American. Arrests: twenty-one, for crimes including attempted rape, breaking and entering, assault with intent to kill, armed robbery, and trafficking in stolen goods. Convictions: two, both for breaking and entering. Served eighteen months in the youth correction center in St. Charles. No known address.

Iago Simms, 14, five feet five, 140 pounds. African-American. Distinguishing characteristics: left side of face sags slightly from nerve damage resulting from a beating from his mother's boyfriend when Simms was six. Arrests: two, for breaking and entering. Convictions: two; remanded to parental custody on both occasions. No time served. Residence: mother's apartment.

"I say we do it," Lonny said, still looking out the window but pulling down his Oakland Raiders cap to emphasize his determination.

"What the hell, you know? We do it," Dalbert said with a shrug.

"What the hell," added Iago. "When?"

"Tomorrow. Why we gotta wait?" asked Dalbert, turning to face his friends.

"That's fresh froze with me," said Dalbert, watching Yogi Bear shoot up on a geyser.

Iago shrugged.

* * *

It was fate, destiny, dumb luck, something. Less than five hours after Abe Lieberman had left his office, Dr. Jacob Berry, late of Lansing, Michigan, had a gun.

The morning schedule had been light. Four uneventful physical exams for police officers, two off-the-street patients, both Vietnamese, one with a severely strained back, the other with cuts on his arm from an exploding jar. Both of the Vietnamese had paid in cash, which, when they left, Jacob Berry had folded and tucked into the pocket of the money strap tied to his ankle and hidden by his sock. Jacob also kept his driver's license, credit cards, and Blue Cross cards in the hidden pocket. In his wallet he kept around fifty dollars, some family photographs, and a few store credit cards from East Lansing. He had purchased the hidden pocket four days after coming to an initial understanding of where his practice was located.

When he had finished patching the arms of the Vietnamese man, who looked ancient and malnourished and communicated through an old woman whose English was incomprehensible, Jacob adjusted his glasses and called his brother.

"Isaac? I'm sending you a police officer named Lieberman, Abraham Lieberman. History of heart disease in the family. High cholesterol and the rest. I'll mail you the file and lab results."

"He calls. We book him. That's our motto," said Isaac abruptly, which was a clear signal to Jacob that his brother had something more important to do than take this call. "Anything else?"

"I can make it for dinner Wednesday."

"Good. Call Jennifer. No, I'll tell her. Seven-thirty if you want to see the kids before they go to bed."

"Seven-thirty, fine."

"Anything else, Jacob?"

"You have a gun, Isaac?"

A short pause and then, "What happened?" Isaac asked.

Jacob looked at the window of his office/examining room. He had kept the blinds closed, a captive of daylight darkness instead of gray spring light.

"This isn't the safest part of the city, Isaac. I took your word, let you . . ."

"We've been through this, Jacob. No place is safe in the city. You go where you can practice and make a living. The worse the neighborhood the more diverse the patient problems."

Jacob did not point out that his brother's practice was in two offices, one on Michigan Avenue and one in Winnetka, reasonably safe from immediate violence.

"I asked you, Isaac. Do you have a gun?"

A beat passed. A sigh and, "Yes. I keep it in my briefcase, put the case on the corner of my desk every morning and next to me in the car. It doesn't go in the house. You're thinking about getting a gun."

Isaac's house was in Kenilworth, the most exclusive and restricted suburb on the Lake Michigan shore.

"I think I should," said Jacob.

"Jake, I don't have time now, but listen. You have police officers coming into your office all day. What better protection could you want?"

"Not all day, Isaac. And they don't go out the door with me. They don't walk me to my car and to my apartment when I get home."

"We'll talk about it Thursday, OK? I really have to go."

"OK," Jacob agreed.

Isaac hung up first.

Jacob Berry took off his blue shirt with the embroidered name and hung it on a hanger in the closet. He left his lights on, moved to the waiting room, went out, and locked his office door behind him. He thought he heard a sound in the darkness of the corridor, near the solid wooden door of A. R. Oriental Imports about a dozen feet away. But no one was there.

He hurried the two short flights down the stairs, took five echoing steps across the cracked white tile floor that was almost exactly like the tiles his mother had in her bathroom, and went into the chilly spring afternoon.

An el train going north toward Evanston had just rattled out of the station. Jacob didn't look up. He passed Vietnamese, whites shopping at the Oriental stores, and a few black men he recognized as working in the neighborhood. His destination was the Solid Blue Diner on the corner of Broadway and Argyle. It was where he ate almost every day. Jacob's digestive tract couldn't take more than one Oriental meal a week and the Solid Blue specialized in solid, tasteless tuna sandwiches, burgers, daily specials, and vegetable soup.

Before he was twenty feet from the door of his office, one of the things he dreaded took place. An ancient Oriental woman with a heavily wrinkled face approached him and said, "You want buy jewelry, watches? Real jade. Cheap jade for your lady?"

Jacob Berry shook his head politely but firmly and moved on. Only half a block to go when an Oriental man of no discernible age, hair slicked back and a cigarette burning in the corner of his mouth, approached on his right.

"Listen," the man whispered. "You doctor. I know. Got lots of things, watches, coffee grinders, hot stuff, you know?"

The man winked when Jacob met his eyes while continuing to walk.

"What you need? What you want?" the man whispered, glancing furtively at passersby. "Silk scarves, pearl-handled knives, finest shirts from Hong Kong, cheap."

"You have a gun?" Jacob asked, surprising himself.

The man stopped and so did Jacob. People moved around them. The man with the cigarette in the corner of his mouth cocked his head to the side and looked at Jacob's eyes.

"No," the man said.

"OK," said Jacob, starting to move away.

"Wait. I don't deal in guns but I know someone who does." The man's accent was gone.

"When and how much?" Jacob asked.

A wide Chrysler almost hit a man jaywalking across Bryn Mawr. The Chrysler's driver hit his horn. The jaywalker, a burly Oriental, smashed his fist down on the

Chrysler's hood, screaming something in Chinese or Vietnamese.

"Why don't you just go buy one at Sears?" the man asked suspiciously.

"It takes time, days. I don't want to wait days."

The Oriental man removed the cigarette from his mouth and said, "In this neighborhood, I don't blame you. Where you heading?"

"Diner," Jacob said.

"Eat slow. Digest your food. I'll see what I can do," the man said, turning his back and moving slowly with the flow of pedestrian traffic.

Jacob got a booth in the rear of the dining room of the Solid Blue Diner, which had gotten its name from the pale blue walls. He ordered a bacon, lettuce, and tomato on white toast, a Greek salad, and a Diet Coke. He had bought a late-edition *Sun-Times* from the machine in front of the diner but he didn't feel like reading it.

The old waitress with an odd walk who always waited on him brought the salad. He ate slowly, trying not to listen to the waitress calling orders and people at other tables bantering, joking, talking about nothing.

He was finished with his sandwich and nursing his Coke after the waitress brought his check when the man he had talked to on the street came in and moved toward him. The man was carrying a small paper bag. He slid into the booth across from Jacob Berry. There was no expression on his face.

"Sixty dollars," the man said softly.

"I've only got fifty-six and I haven't paid for my lunch."

"Fifty dollars," the man sighed in resignation, looking around the diner and out the window where pedestrians passed, paying no attention.

"Take the bag," the man said.

Jacob reached under the table and took the crumpled brown bag. Something felt cool and heavy inside it.

"Money," the man said.

Jacob took out his wallet and counted out three tens and a twenty. The man took the money above the table, counted it, and stuffed it into his pocket. He looked around again and started to get up.

"Wait," Jacob said. "I've never shot a gun."

"Simple," whispered the man, leaning over the table toward Jacob. "It has bullets in it. No safety. Trigger is firm, won't go off by accident. You aim. You shoot. Just like Clint Eastwood. Your day is made."

And the man was gone.

It was over. Just like that. That fast. Wish for something and it appears. If Lieberman called him or mentioned the gun business the next time he saw him, Jacob would do exactly what Lieberman wanted, go through the process of getting a legal gun, and when he had it he would throw the weapon in the brown paper bag away. Meanwhile, he would have a small sense of security.

He stuffed the bag and the gun into his pocket and left the diner. It would be easier to face the afternoon with the weapon in his desk drawer.

"What have we got, Father Murphy?" Lieberman asked when his partner slid into the passenger seat and closed the door.

The seat was already adjusted back so that Bill Hanrahan could stretch his legs and accommodate his football lineman frame.

Bill Hanrahan's hair was growing back with a vengeance. For about six months he had worn his dark hair short and brushed straight back and military. For about the same period he had been on the wagon, tempted but still riding and clinging for dear life to a fender. His face was less red and puffy than it had been when he drank, but there was a recent grayness to his skin and he wore a shave not quite close enough, a tie not fully knotted and not exactly matching his jacket.

"Very little but a corpse, a grieving husband, a preliminary medical, a murder weapon. Least that's what I got from Briggs. Report from Homicide'll be waiting at Rozier's house."

"Grieving husband has clout."

"Meaning?"

"He asks for a specific cop, me, and someone tells Briggs to give the man what he wants," said Lieberman.

"Reads that way, Abe."

"We shall see, Father Murphy. We shall see."

They were driving away from Hanrahan's house on a side street in Ravenswood less than two blocks from the Ravenswood Hospital. Bill Hanrahan and his wife, Maureen, had raised two boys in the house. When they were grown and gone, Maureen packed her bags and went on her way. Hanrahan had been through much in the house since then, including his killing of a psycho less than a month ago, a psycho whose wife and young son he'd taken in. The psycho, Frankie Kraylaw, a rifle in his hand, had broken in, demanding his wife. Bill Hanrahan shot him.

The memories had been tainted, but Hanrahan held on, keeping the place in perfect order for the day that Maureen came back, not to stay but to pick something up or just drop in. She would see how well he was doing, how he was straight and sober, how he could make it on his own.

Bill Hanrahan had come to reasonable terms with his life. Three decades ago Hardrock Hanrahan had been the fastest lineman on the Chicago Vocational High School football team. Dick Butkus, who had graduated from CVS a few years after Hanrahan, told Bill at a reunion that Hardrock had been an inspiration to him. And then the knee went in a practice game and so did the speed and any chance at Notre Dame or Illinois or even Wisconsin. He lasted two years at Southern Illinois University and then gave up to join his father as a Chicago cop, as his father had joined his grandfather before him.

Then Maureen came, and the boys and the bottle.

But things were better now. He even went to Saint Bart's once in awhile, though not recently, and he was engaged to a Chinese woman named Iris Chen. A new start. Who knows?

Hanrahan had received a phone call the night before on his unlisted phone, a phone call from a man with just the hint of an Oriental accent. The man said he was calling for

47

Mr. Woo. The man paused to see if Hanrahan recognized the name. He did.

"Mr. Woo, as you know, is a very influential and civic-minded businessman," the man said.

Laio Woo, Hanrahan knew, owned about a quarter of Chinatown and had a piece of most Chinese-owned businesses in the city. He was also suspected of cooperating with a major narcotics operation to the Midwest out of Hong Kong. The mayor took pictures with him and shook his hand. Civic organizations honored him for his generous contributions. Those who knew better kept their mouths shut.

"I'm aware of that," Hanrahan said.

"The Chen family is very dear to Mr. Woo. His father knew them well in China many years ago. He has been, as he has to many in our community, a benevolent patron to the Chens. You understand?"

"I'm with you," said Hanrahan.

"Mr. Woo thinks it would be best if Iris Chen married within her own culture."

"He does?"

"Yes."

"You know I'm a cop?"

"Of course," the man said calmly. "And Mr Woo is aware that you are divorced, are alcoholic, and have been disciplined twice by the department for misconduct. Mr. Woo would be very grateful if you would simply cease your relationship with Miss Chen."

"Grateful, how grateful?" Hanrahan asked.

The man on the phone sighed.

"Please, Mr. Hanrahan, we are not fools. You will be offered no money. Mr. Woo is well aware that such an offer might be illegal and that you most certainly would not accept it."

"You know what you can tell Mr. Woo?"

"Yes, I know the limits of that which I can convey to him."

"If Iris Chen wants to marry me, then I'm doing it. And

48

I'd advise Mr. Woo not to do anything that sounds to me like he's putting pressure on Miss Chen. You understand?"

"Clearly," said the man. "But can you not see the merit of Mr. Woo's concern?"

Neither Iris nor her father had ever mentioned Woo.

Hanrahan hung up. Partly out of simple anger. Partly because he did see the merit in Woo's concern.

Lieberman was fully aware that his partner was lost in thought on the inside and slipping on the outside.

"I'm fine, Rabbi," he said as they turned west on Wilson. "Did I ask?"

"Didn't have to," said Hanrahan, shifting his weight. "I'm still straight and sober."

"Which is more than can be said for most of the world."

"Amen."

Traffic cones let them know they were approaching a school crossing. Lieberman slowed down. A thin man with a white beard stepped into the crosswalk and held up his hand for Lieberman to stop. A gaggle of small children scurried across.

"My boys used to cross here," Hanrahan said. "One of the reasons we moved here in the first place. Decent school, short walk. How's Lisa?"

The crossing guard stepped to the curb and Lieberman touched the gas pedal gently.

"She's fine. Getting used to the idea that Todd's going to marry the teacher."

"She'll be moving out?"

"No sign, but Bess is matchmaking with the fury of no mean proportions. And I've got my eye on a promising doctor."

"Life is hard, Rabbi."

"Life is hard, Father Murph, but it has its compensations, including . . ."

"The Cubbies—"

"Maish's corned beef and chopped liver with a new pickle—"

"The kids—"

"The job—"

49

They turned at Western Avenue and went north. Traffic was light.

"Coffee?" Lieberman asked.

"I won't turn it down."

Lieberman turned on the radio, found the oldies station, and headed for Dunkin' Donuts. They drove silently, listening to Benny Goodman, Nat King Cole, Teresa Brewer, and Kitty Kallen. They drove past car dealers, a spotting of McDonald'ses, a forest of video shops, upholsterers, supermarkets, and a plethora of liquor stores.

"You know the new doc, Berry?" said Lieberman. "He's the possible for Lisa."

"Heard about him, that's all."

"What'd you hear?"

Hanrahan looked at his partner as Ginny Simms sang "These Foolish Things."

"He's Jewish, name's Berry."

"That I know," said Lieberman. "Tell me what I don't know."

"Came from Ohio."

"Michigan," Lieberman corrected.

"Ah," said Hanrahan, shifting to face his partner.

"My daughter needs a life," said Lieberman. "My grandchildren need a home, not a campsite in their grandparents' hovel. I need my house back. Lisa and Doc Berry are a perfect match. He's easy to push around and has even less of a sense of humor than Lisa."

"Sounds made in heaven."

"He likes the Cubs," Lieberman said.

"Good."

"Chance in a thousand, but who knows?"

They pulled into the Dunkin' Donuts. Lieberman went in and came out with coffee and a donut, chocolate frosted, and a folded copy of the *Chicago Tribune*.

"You're not having donuts?" Hanrahan asked, taking the newspaper and opening the bag.

"Rozier, Rozier," Lieberman said, nodding the question away and changing the subject. "Can't place him. They sure it was me he asked for?"

"Lieberman, Abe," said Hanrahan, scanning the front page of the paper and trying not to spill his coffee. "That's what Gibbs said. Here it is. Page one, but at the bottom. Photo of Rozier and his wife."

"And . . ."

"Let's see. Ah, the answer to your question. Harvey Rozier is, and I quote, 'the prominent financial adviser to many of the county's elite, including Judges O'Donald, Hershkowitz, Balziniak, and Lincoln. Other clients include'—let's see who's interesting. I think this is the short list. A handful of corporate types and the president of the University of Chicago."

"What else?"

"Short article, but pretty much what Gibbs said on the phone. Wife was feeling sick. Usual night to go to a concert with friends. She insisted that Rozier go without her. He went. Came back with the friends and found what was left of Dana Rozier and a lot of blood. That's about it."

"TV pick it up?" Lieberman asked, trying to ignore the smell of Hanrahan's donut.

"Don't know. Happened late. Didn't watch this morning."

"They'll be there," Lieberman said. "Suggestion, Father Murph."

"Fire," said Hanrahan.

"Use your comb, fix your tie, and use the electric razor inside the glove compartment."

Fifteen minutes later, empty cups and waxed paper stuffed into the bright donut bag, they pulled up to the entrance to the driveway of the Rozier house, where three private security guards in gray Kleinert Security uniforms were holding curious neighbors and impatient television crews at bay.

Lieberman flashed his badge. One of the uniformed guards nodded and they parted to let him drive through to the house, where two more uniformed Kleinert guards protected the door.

"Five to one Andy Kleinert is a Rozier client," said Hanrahan as they got out of the car.

Lieberman nodded. He was thinking about donuts.

Hanrahan reached for his badge, but one of the guards, a hefty man with cropped red hair, held up his hand.

"I know who you are. How've you been, Abe?"

He held out his hand, and Lieberman took it.

"Breathing," said Lieberman. "This is my partner, Bill Hanrahan. Scotty Phierson."

Phierson took Hanrahan's hand.

"Scotty worked the Lawndale," Abe said. "Hard times in the mill."

"Hard times indeed. Then my heart had enough. But I got no complaints, Abraham. Pay's good. Work's easy. Just got to dress up like a mailman once in a while. But the material's good. Feel it."

Lieberman touched the uniform and wondered how he would look in one. He concluded quickly that his effect would be decidedly comic.

"Good fabric," said Lieberman.

"First class," said Phierson, opening the door and leading the two detectives inside.

"Ask me a question, Abe," Phierson said quietly when the door was closed. "Company rule: don't volunteer. But you ask me a question, I've got to answer."

"What do you know the *Tribune* doesn't?" Lieberman asked.

"Not much. Homicide came in around one in the morning. We got here about an hour later."

"Who called you?" Hanrahan asked.

"Boss. Kleinert himself. The old boy. Two in the morning. Mr. Harvey Rozier knows the right people. What was left of the lady's body was taken out a few minutes after we got here. Evidence truck was here till about an hour, hour and a half ago."

"No cleanup?" Lieberman said, looking at the blood spots on the tile and steps that had been carefully outlined with white adhesive tape.

"None. That's about all I know. You want to see Rozier and his lawyer now? They're upstairs. Said you should come right up."

"Lawyer?" asked Hanrahan, looking at his partner.

"And best friend. Ken Franklin. You know the name?"

"We know the name," Hanrahan said with a sigh.

"Let's take a look at the kitchen before we go up," said Lieberman.

Phierson led the way, being careful not to step into any of the neatly marked splotches and splatters of Dana Rozier's blood.

When they stepped into the kitchen there were few places to stand that weren't splattered with blood. The outline of a body in tape lay next to the back door.

"Phone cord was cut clean," Phierson said. "Saw the body. That was one crazy hophead, you ask me. But don't quote me on it."

"Too damn many bloody footprints," Hanrahan said.

"What do you make of that, Murph?" said Lieberman.

Hanrahan followed his partner's eyes to a patch of blood.

"Looks like the blood flowed around something, Rabbi. Over there. Block of wood maybe. Maybe Evidence took it."

"Only thing I saw them take out was a set of kitchen knives," said Phierson.

Hanrahan took notes in his book. Lieberman made his way on tiptoe to the pantry and opened it. Cans, cereal, boxes were lined up neatly on white shelves except for one shelf about shoulder high. The boxes on that shelf were out of line and one of them looked as if it were about to fall to the floor.

"We'll come back," he said, stepping out of the pantry.

They followed Phierson back through the kitchen door, past the dining room, and up the stairs. There were more patches of blood on the stairs, right up to the landing and beyond.

"No blood in any of the bedrooms," said Phierson. "Ask me, she heard the guy. He thought the place was empty, spotted her up here, grabbed a knife out of the kitchen, came up here, and—"

Phierson had stopped in front of a door at the end of the inlaid wood floor. He knocked.

"Come in," a man said. And in they went.

"What took you so long?" a man Lieberman's age dressed in a business suit said, checking his watch.

The Usual Suspects

At the moment Hanrahan and Lieberman were entering the study of Harvey Rozier, Dr. Jacob Berry was standing inside the outer door of his office trying to decide whether or not to open the door to the man with the booming, angry voice.

"Hey, I know you in there. What the fuck, man? I got a 'mergency here."

Jacob went back to his office and got the new gun out of the drawer. It felt cool and lighter than he had imagined. He put the gun in his pocket, which sagged suspiciously under its weight, and moved back into the reception room, where he opened the outer door with a trembling hand.

Two men burst in, both black, one in his forties or fifties, big, the other young and slender with a frightened look on his face. They were wearing jeans and matching orange shirts.

Jacob came very near to shooting them.

And then he saw that the young man was bleeding, his left hand a deep, moist red.

"What you all doin' in here? Playin' with yourself? Got a man here bleedin' to death," the big man said angrily.

"This way," Jacob said, leading them into the office/examining room.

"My son, Jamie here, caught it in the truck door. We was unloading fish at the Chink restaurant downstairs."

Jamie was beyond discussing anything. He was biting his lower lip so hard that Jacob had to tell him to open his mouth and take deep breaths. Jamie, little more than a scared boy, nodded and tried. His breaths were not deep but his mouth was open.

Jacob sat him on the examining table and told the father to be sure his son didn't fall off. Then Jacob washed his hands in the sink and examined the damage.

Jamie was holding his left wrist with his right. He held it away from his body. His shirt was already badly stained. Jamie made small whimpering sounds as Jacob carefully cleaned the hand, probing for broken bones and looking for lacerations.

"Not too bad," Jacob said. "From the swelling and tenderness I'd say the middle finger is broken. Looks like a simple fracture, but he'll have to have X rays. I'll clean the wounds, give him something for the pain and something to hold his hand steady till you get him to the emergency room. You know where Weiss Hospital is? It's just—"

"I know," said the older man. "I don't have much cash on me. You take a check?"

"Can you manage ten dollars cash or a check for twenty-five?"

"Yeah. Cash."

"I don't think the lacerations need suturing, but that's something for the ER," said Jacob. "Don't worry. He's going to be fine. My advice is that you and Jamie wear thick gloves when you work."

"Thanks, Doc," the older man said, clearly relieved and touching his son on the cheek. "Now, you min' if I give you some advice?"

"No," said Jacob, working on the wounded hand.

"Get yourself a holster for that thing in your pocket," the big man said. "The way you carryin', some bad ass is gonna figure you got something to protect."

Harvey Rozier's study was as big as Lieberman's living room. No, it was bigger, and certainly better furnished. One row of books, colorful Oriental rug on the inlaid wood floor, antique French desk near the floor-length windows, a green wing-backed chair and two-seat couch that perfectly matched the dominant colors of the rug and the muted green of the wall. Three movie posters were framed on the wall, from *King Kong*, *Casablanca*, and *Gone With the Wind*. Lieberman would have bet his house that all three were originals.

And then there were the two men. Kenneth Franklin was standing, impatient. He was tall, tan, and athletic-club trim, and in better shape than Lieberman, who was younger. Harvey Rozier had been sitting at the end of the couch. He got up slowly and held out his hand. He wasn't conspicuously built like a bodybuilder, but it was clear that he was in good condition. His dark, not-too-long hair was combed neatly back and he looked as if he had recently shaved. He wore jeans, a perfectly ironed tan Burberry shirt, and sneakers.

"Thank you for coming, Detectives," Rozier said sincerely, shaking their hands and meeting their eyes. "Please make yourselves comfortable. There's a small refrigerator in the master bedroom if you'd like something light to drink."

Harvey Rozier's eyes were red and moist. He rubbed his hands together as if they were cold and sat back down in the corner of the couch.

"Gentlemen," Franklin said. "Considering what Mr. Rozier has been through, we would appreciate it if you could keep this brief. We, and my wife, have already given a full account to the detectives who came last night, or this morning, if we are going to be precise. Neither Mr. Rozier nor I have had any rest—"

"It's all right, Ken," Rozier said, his right hand covering his eyes. "I want to talk to these men. I want whoever did that to Dana to be caught soon, tried quickly, and put away forever."

Ken Franklin shrugged in resignation and sat next to Harvey Rozier.

Hanrahan leaned back against the bookcase, where he could watch the men and admire the posters. Lieberman took the wing-backed chair.

"I understand you asked for me by name. Why?" asked Lieberman.

Harvey Rozier looked up.

"Someone told me you were the best," he said.

"I'll be content with 'one of the best,' " said Lieberman. "Who?"

"Is this really—" Franklin said, but Rozier held up his hand to stop him.

"Ida Katzman," Rozier said. "I handle her accounts and coordinate her investments. She's mentioned you more than once."

Mystery explained, in a way. Ida Katzman was eighty-six years old, walked with a cane, and had a seat in the front room of Temple Mir Shavot, where Bess Lieberman was president. Ida Katzman was the principal donor to the temple and the primary source of funding for the new temple on Dempster, now being remodeled from a Great National Bank. Ida was the widow of Mort, who had died more than twenty years ago. He had come to Chicago with then-borrowed dollars and gone to his grave owning ten very successful jewelry stores in ten major cities. It was all Ida's now. There was nothing wrong with Ida Katzman's business judgment. In the two decades since her husband's death, Ida, apparently with the advice of Harvey Rozier, had doubled the number of stores and, it was rumored by none other than Rabbi Wass himself, the young Rabbi Wass, that she had more than doubled the company's net worth.

"I'll thank Mrs. Katzman when I see her at services Friday," Lieberman said.

Rozier examined Lieberman's face for a tint of sarcasm, but there was none there. Hanrahan had his notebook out.

"Would you ask your friend to please not lean against the bookcase?" Franklin said.

"Detective Hanrahan," Lieberman said, cocking his head toward his partner. "Would you please not lean against the bookcase?"

Hanrahan took a half step forward.

"Mr. Rozier," Lieberman continued. "I think I would like a glass of water."

Rozier started to rise, but Franklin put out a hand to stop him.

"I'll get it," he said. "And you?"

"Nothing for me," said Hanrahan.

"If it's not too much trouble, Ken," Rozier said, "I'd like a mineral water too."

Ken Franklin nodded and went out the door. Lieberman launched immediately into his questions after asking if it was all right to tape the conversation. Rozier said it was.

LIEBERMAN: Why didn't your wife go to the, what was it . . . ?

ROZIER: Chamber music. We have series tickets with the Franklins. Every Tuesday. Dana was a little sick to her stomach. I think it was from the fish we had at dinner. I wasn't feeling too well either, but nothing like Dana. I wish I had been sicker. I wish . . . but Dana insisted that I go.

LIEBERMAN: You were all together, you and the Franklins, from the time you left the house till the time you came back through the front door?

ROZIER: I don't . . .

LIEBERMAN: I'd like to eliminate you from suspicion fast, before the papers or channel 4 start exercising their imagination.

ROZIER: I see. Of course. The husband is the first suspect. We all went into the concert together at eight, had drinks at intermission around nine. I went to the rest room just as intermission ended. Gone, I don't know, five minutes, maybe less. Other than that . . .

LIEBERMAN: When did you go to the rest room?

ROZIER: God, I don't . . . Yes, just before the Vivaldi piece. Got back in time to hear most of it. Cello, I remember, went a little flat in the scherzo.

LIEBERMAN:	That a fact? You were seen during the performance by the Franklins, then?
ROZIER:	And many others, too.

Ken Franklin returned and placed a tray with two fluted glasses on the small wooden table.

"Quibel," he said, handing a glass to Lieberman and to Rozier before checking the crease in his trousers and sitting.

Man's got style, Lieberman thought and then asked . . .

LIEBERMAN:	Mr. Franklin, you were in sight of Mr. Rozier throughout the concert?
FRANKLIN:	What the hell do you—?
ROZIER:	It's all right, Ken. He's doing his job.
FRANKLIN:	Yes.
LIEBERMAN:	Did he leave the room during the performance?
FRANKLIN:	I don't know. Perhaps for a minute or two. No, he did leave for a few minutes to use the rest room at the end of the intermission.
LIEBERMAN:	You saw him come back into the hall?
FRANKLIN:	Don't remember, but I do recall looking back at Mr. Rozier once or twice after the intermission. Does that satisfy you?
LIEBERMAN:	You remember the Vivaldi piece?
FRANKLIN:	This is . . . Yes.
LIEBERMAN:	Mr. Rozier tells me the violin was a bit off on the scherzo.
FRANKLIN:	For God's sake. Dana was murdered, horribly . . . and you . . . All right. No, the violin was fine. The girl on the cello was definitely off on that piece. Now if—
LIEBERMAN:	Any of you touch anything when you came in and found Mrs. Rozier's body?
ROZIER:	I . . . went to Dana, lifted her head, knew she was dead, but . . .
LIEBERMAN:	Touched nothing?
ROZIER:	Not that I recall.

FRANKLIN: Nor I, nor Mrs. Franklin. I said immediately that nothing should be touched.

LIEBERMAN: We'll check with the neighbors, but did you see anyone unfamiliar in the neighborhood in the last week or two? Your wife mention anyone?

ROZIER: No, I don't think . . . God, there was a man, came to the door last Sunday. Wanted to know if we needed a handyman. Said he had a customer in the neighborhood and was trying to pick up more work. But I don't think . . .

LIEBERMAN: He give you a card? His name?

ROZIER: No, maybe. Maybe he did mumble it. I told him immediately that we've had the same handyman, Jeff Lerner, for years. He does electrical work, carpentry, a little plumbing.

LIEBERMAN: Didn't say which neighbor he was working for?

ROZIER: No.

LIEBERMAN: Think you'd recognize him again if you saw him?

ROZIER: Absolutely.

FRANKLIN: Harvey has an amazing memory for faces, names, and numbers.

LIEBERMAN: Good. Would you mind coming to the station and looking at some pictures?

FRANKLIN: You mean now?

LIEBERMAN: The closer we are to the event, the more likely you are to recognize him. We can wait till—

ROZIER: I'll be happy to come whenever you like, the sooner the better. Now is fine. If he . . . Ken, I know you're tired, but if you can hold down the fort for another hour or so . . .

FRANKLIN: Of course.

LIEBERMAN: Good. Then let's go. And thanks for the water.

They didn't have to say anything. Hanrahan simply stayed outside to follow up with the neighbors when Abe and Rozier got into Lieberman's car.

"Back here in front of the house in two hours," Lieberman said.

"Cutting it close for the Cubbies," Hanrahan said quietly.

"Tomorrow," said Lieberman, "Giants are in town."

Cameras turned and reporters with microphones shouted questions through the closed window, but Lieberman had no trouble getting through on a path cleared by Scotty Phierson and his Kleinert crew.

Lieberman looked up at the window of Rozier's study. Kenneth Franklin looked down at the policeman. The old lawyer didn't look quite so health-club robust from this angle. Lieberman backed out, leaving his partner in the driveway.

Lieberman drove silently, heading back toward the heart of the city.

"Radio all right?" asked Lieberman, Rozier at his side.

The smell of donuts and coffee hung in the car. Abe Lieberman's stomach growled.

Rozier nodded. Lieberman turned the radio on and pushed the button for the oldies station. Rudy Vallee was looking for a nasal high note in "Goodnight Sweetheart."

"Kids?" asked Lieberman.

Rozier shook his head no.

"Wife's relatives? Yours?"

"Dana's parents live in Santa Fe. I talked to them earlier. They'll be here sometime tonight or this afternoon."

". . . till we meet tomorrow," Rudy crooned.

"No brothers, sisters, cousins?"

"Dana's father said he'd take care of that. One brother. A few cousins I've never met. My parents are dead. I was an only child. Haven't talked to my aunt and cousins in, who knows, twenty-five years. Ken and Betty are the closest thing I have to family. I'm sorry, but do you mind changing the station?"

"No," said Lieberman, even though they both knew that he did.

A classical piece came on and Rozier closed his eyes.

"I've had a few tranquilizers," Rozier said.

"I understand."

Nothing more was said till they pulled into the small parking lot behind the Clark Street Station. The smell of the Wendy's next to the station hit Abe when he opened the car door. It made him long for a burger with fries even though he ate at fast-food restaurants only in emergencies. Home or Maish's T & L were the places of choice. He would have to read carefully the brochures Doc Berry had given him. He would have to tell Bess tonight and they would have to come up with a plan that would keep Abe from temptation. It was going to be hard. A good pastrami on fresh rye with a pickle was the best refuge from the chaos of human existence. He would have to make an effort this time and stick to the diet.

Lieberman led Rozier down the cement path to the front of the station and into the lobby, where Sergeant Nestor Briggs was on the desk talking to a pair of women complaining in Spanish, a language that had successfully eluded Nestor in his almost thirty years as a Chicago cop. Nestor looked more than a little like Edgar Kennedy, the old-time bald actor who did a slow burn at the antics of every comic from Keaton to Abbott and Costello. Not only was Briggs trying to handle the complaint, he was also trying to deal with a phone call. He barely nodded as Lieberman and Rozier went by.

Tapes and mug books were kept in the "library," through the doors behind Nestor Briggs. Abe led Rozier to the small room, sat him at a table in front of a computer screen, and said, "Gonna show you burglars, hundreds of burglars, but we'll try to narrow it down so you don't start forgetting his face."

"I'll recognize him if I see him," said Rozier.

"Right," said Lieberman. "The memory. Can I get you a Coke, coffee, something?"

"Coke, diet, with caffeine."

Lieberman picked up the phone on the table and hit two buttons.

"Bobby, you got someone up there can bring a Coke, diet, with caffeine, and a coffee, black, with even more caffeine, down to the library?"

"You got Rozier down there?" asked Bobby Arango.

"Yes," said Abe.

"Then I'll be right down. I want to get a look. Morbid, huh?" asked Arango. "You think he whacked her, paid someone to do it?"

"Bobby, one Coke, one coffee, no questions," said Lieberman.

"You got it. Guess who we got up here?"

"Maury Povich," said Lieberman, looking at Rozier.

"Come on, get real, Abe," sighed Arango.

"Wilma Rudolph."

"Who's Wilma . . . ?"

"Who've you got, Officer Arango?"

"Chuculo Fernandez," Bobby answered.

"Charges?"

"Ghost rider on a Clark Street bus wreck. He was with a new girl, Leona something. Seems he wanted to play rough after the event. Celebrate his good luck. She didn't want to."

"And?"

"They played rough," said Bobby. "She turned him in on the ghost scam when Fernandez put her in the hospital."

"How badly is she hurt?" Lieberman asked, looking at Rozier, who was looking out the window at a rapidly graying day.

"Not too bad. She'll live. Want to talk to Fernandez? He asked for you."

"Later. Coffee and Coke, Bobby," Lieberman reminded and hung up.

Chuculo Fernandez was a member of the Tentáculos, a Hispanic gang headed by a madman, Emiliano Del Sol, who had a decidedly uncharacteristic fondness for Lieberman. Chuculo was stupid and quick with his knife. The Tentáculos were Mexicans, Guatemalans, and Panamanians led by the almost legendary El Perro, Emiliano Del Sol. El Perro was reported to have killed more than one man—

always men—for looking at or seeming to look at the scar on his cheek for too long.

Even a turn-away judge like Mitgang would have trouble giving Fernandez less than two years plus, even with a crime like ghost riding.

Ghost riders are a big-city phenomenon—New York, Chicago, L.A., Detroit. Nothing new. A man or a woman with a criminal heart happens to be lucky enough to be on the scene when a bus gets in a wreck or four or five cars pile up. Our criminal heart joins the jolted passengers and claims he or she was on the bus and is dying of internal injuries. Four lawyers with police band radios are usually on the spot as fast as the police are, picking up clients. Sometimes, if they get there before the police, the lawyer will even join the jolted and claim he or she was on the bus. A felony. Not a big one, but a felony.

Lieberman turned to the computer and flipped a switch.

They went through two tapes with about eighty faces on each. Three times Rozier paused at pictures, all somewhat similar, thin white males in their forties. Each time he paused, Rozier asked the name of the person in the picture. None of the names rang a bell.

Bobby Arango came in with the drinks, gawked discreetly, and exited professionally.

Rozier stopped at two more mug shots in the thick book that Lieberman then placed in front of him, asked their names, and said they were close but he was sure they weren't the one.

It was a game now and it was over. The third picture on the videotape had been Gregor Eupatniaks, a.k.a. George Patniks, a.k.a. Pitty-Pitty Patniks. Rozier had asked for no more information than the name of the man who had seen him murder his wife.

"I'm sorry," Rozier said an hour and another Coke and coffee later, when they closed the final book.

"That's all right," said Lieberman. "They come in all the time. We'll keep checking. He may be new at this or new in town."

Lieberman had made a note of each man Rozier had considered.

"I think I'd like to go back home now," said Rozier, rising and rubbing his forehead.

"Let's go, and thanks for your cooperation."

"You're welcome."

"We'll catch him, Mr. Rozier. I've got a feeling he made a lot of mistakes. You don't just break into a house, panic, murder, and run without leaving something."

"I hope you're right," said Harvey Rozier. "I hope to God you're right."

"I've got to make one quick stop upstairs before we go. Do you mind?"

"I'll just stay here if it's all right," said Rozier. "I wouldn't mind being alone for a few minutes."

Lieberman nodded, went into the narrow hall and up the flight of steps to the squad room. Everyone called it the squad room, though there were no squads. It was just what you called the room where the detectives had their desks, took their calls, got their assignments, and brought suspects, victims, and witnesses.

Joe Wiznicki was at his desk, rubbing his mouth and pecking out a report on his computer. "Black and White," Applegate and Acardo, hovered over a skinny woman clutching her purse in her lap. Probably a victim. In the corner, near the windows that were designed never to open, sat a handcuffed Chuculo Fernandez, a thin, surly twenty-year-old with a long record of violence and the distinction of being one of the three craziest members of the Tentáculos.

Ernest Cadwell was talking to Fernandez, who, slumped in his chair, hat Sinatra style over his brow, was doing his best to look bored. Cadwell, a huge black man with a patience Lieberman admired but couldn't understand, was calmly asking Fernandez questions in a combination of English and Spanish.

"Viejo," Fernandez said, seeing Lieberman.

"*Muy lejos de su país,* Chuculo," said Lieberman.

"*Pues . . .*"

"*Dígame, ¿qué pasa?* In English," said Lieberman.

"There was this *puta*, you know?" Chuculo said, slowly sitting up and tilting his hat back on his head. "I pay her good. She say OK, Chico. We fuck. Then she call a cop and they pick me up in front of some bar a block away. That sound like someone running?"

"You hit the woman, Fernandez."

"A little, maybe," he shrugged.

"Broken right cheek bone, lacerations around the eye requiring suturing, bruised ribs, and a nasty bite on her left ear," said Cadwell matter-of-factly.

"Hey, Viejo, you remember how it is," Fernandez explained. "Passion. You get carried away."

"She says you were ghost riding," said Lieberman.

"Nunca," said Fernandez with indignation. "Never in my life."

"Battery and ghost riding, Chuculo. You're in for a long day. *Mucho gusto de verle a usted, otra vez,* Fernandez," Lieberman said, turning his back.

"Wait, hold it," said Fernandez, starting to get up. Cadwell reached over, grabbed the young man's shoulder, and calmly pushed him back down.

"Viejo, you go see Emiliano," Fernandez said. "He'll make you a deal."

"When I have some time," Lieberman said, walking away.

When Lieberman got back to the library, Harvey Rozier, apparently lost in his nightmare, looked up at him.

"We can go now. Sorry," said Lieberman.

Rozier shook his head and smiled understandingly.

They drove back to Rozier's house in silence. Not even the radio. The sky was sunless and gray, as it had been for days, and the rain was back, light but certain.

Lieberman was sure of one thing. He didn't like Harvey Rozier. Maybe it was class envy or that Rozier reminded him of some almost-forgotten enemy in high school or the way Rozier looked as if he were struggling to contain his grief. Or maybe Lieberman was wrong. It wasn't necessarily a meaningful observation. Abe had known victims who deserved shooting and no sympathy and he had known and liked more than one murderer.

Lieberman would do his job. And it looked like he would miss the Cubs, at least today. Hell, it would probably be rained out anyway.

Houses

The game wasn't rained out. There were two delays but they rushed it through between cloudbursts. The Pirates were up four to two in the top of the seventh when Lieberman and Hanrahan came in the door of the T & L Deli on Devon.

On the radio, Harry Carey was exhorting the crowd.

"Let me hear ya," he cried, and the crowd came back with "Take Me Out to the Ball Game."

At their reserved front table, the only table in the T & L, three of the Alter Cocker regulars—Herschel Rosen, Syd Levan, and Howie Chen—kept singing along with Harry when the policemen entered. There was a fourth man at the table who wasn't singing, but he was smiling knowingly and nodding his head.

Syd Levan, the youngest Cocker at sixty-eight, motioned to Lieberman and Hanrahan to stop at their table. They did and dutifully waited till "Root, root, root for the Cubbies" let the patrons of the T & L, including two women at the counter and a couple with a small child in one of the red leatherette booths, know that the important part was coming.

"For it's one, two, three strikes you're out at the old ball game," the three Cockers and the little boy in the booth belted out.

Syd, always jaunty, a retired insurance salesman, in a yellow sweater, held up a hand to let Herschel introduce the new man. Hersch, who was seventy-one, was a retired jewelry salesman. He had been "Red" Rosen back in the late thirties when Marshall High School went on a hundred-

69

game winning streak. There were people who still recognized the name, though the white hair held only a hint of red-orange. Hersch was the acknowledged leader of the Alter Cockers, the wit, the one with the most moxie and the biggest reputation.

"Detectives Lieberman and Hanrahan," Herschel Rosen said somberly, "I want you to meet a new member of our table, Morris Becker. Morris was telling us just before you came in that he didn't know if he should be carrying a couple of ounces of heroin in his pocket. He's from Saint Louis, where they let old farts get away with anything."

"No," Morris Becker cried, suddenly standing up and almost knocking over what looked like a glass of cherry seltzer.

Becker was frail, thin, and, in spite of a green jacket and a matching beret, less than a monument to free spirithood.

"No," Becker repeated, looking at Herschel Rosen with disbelief. "I never . . . As God is my witness. On the grave of my father, *aleh vei sholom*, I've never . . ."

"Herschel's joking," said Howie Chen. "He's getting a distorted idea of humor since he's gone senile."

Howie, the only non-Jew in the Cockers, was also the oldest at eighty-two, though he looked two decades younger. Howie had owned the Blue Dragon Restaurant a block away, working fourteen to eighteen hours a day for more than thirty years. When he retired and left the restaurant to his grandson, he had been welcomed to the table. Outside of Herschel and Morrie Stoltzer, Howie spoke the best Yiddish of all the Cockers.

"Abe, tell him," Howie said.

"It's a joke, Mr. Becker," Lieberman said, holding out his hand.

"Then you're not the police," Becker said, slowly putting out his right hand, half expecting it to be grasped and the cuffs snapped in place like on television.

"We are the police," said Hanrahan, "but we know Mr. Rosen. You're being initiated."

"Pleased to meet you," said Becker, shaking hands and sitting back down with a suspicious glance at Herschel.

"Al and Morrie?" asked Lieberman.

"The atheists are in traffic court," explained Howie Chen. "Al backed into Morrie in the parking lot and—"

"No, no, no," Herschel groaned. "Morrie backed into Al."

"It makes a difference?" Howie asked, looking to Lieberman for help.

"It makes a major difference here," Herschel insisted. "What are you talkin'? In China it might not make a difference. Here it makes a difference."

Howie Chen had never been in China. He was born in San Francisco. Herschel had come to the United States in 1931. It gave Howie about three years longer in America.

"Anyway," Howie went on, "they face each other in traffic court this afternoon. We're waiting for the winner to come and crow."

Al Bloombach and Morrie Stoltzer were best friends, had been for almost seventy years. They were also known as the atheist contingent of the Alter Cockers. And, in spite of their shared conviction that there was no deity, they fought over almost every other issue.

The rear booth near the kitchen was free. The detectives moved to it and slid in facing each other. The little boy with his parents at the next booth had heard the two men introduced as policemen. He was standing on his seat and looking back at Lieberman, who opened his jacket to reveal his holster. The boy's eyes widened. Lieberman winked and turned his attention to Hanrahan, who had pulled out his notebook.

There was a poster on the wall above the booth. The faded colors oozed with the call of a Vienna red hot drenched in mustard, onion, tomato, and relish. Lieberman tried not to look.

Manuel, the cook, who normally stayed in the kitchen handling short orders, brought Abe and Bill cups of coffee.

"Where's Maish?" asked Lieberman.

"Your brother's walking," said Manuel, a lean black man in his late forties. Lieberman had put Manuel away on a series of car thefts in 1967. When he got out of prison, where he learned to cook, Lieberman introduced him to Maish, who hired him immediately. That was over twenty-two years ago.

"He does that a lot these days," Manuel continued.

Lieberman nodded.

Maish's son, a rising television executive, had been gunned down in a senseless robbery two months ago. Maish, known throughout his sixty-five years as the dead-pan Nothing Bothers Maish, had been badly shaken. Maish had given his life to his wife, Yetta, his son, and his deli. Now he took long walks to who knew where and showed little interest in the business.

"How about a corned beef, slice of sweet onion on fresh rye, small chopped liver or kishke on the side?" Manuel recommended.

Hanrahan nodded yes, and Lieberman said, "Just a bagel, toasted, with maybe a little jam, jelly, something."

Manuel shrugged and went to take some cash from the two women at the counter who were standing near the cash register.

"You feelin' OK, Rabbi?" Hanrahan asked.

"Diet again, the new doctor. Cholesterol. Don't ask. You, you had your cholesterol checked?"

"Yeah, last year. Levels are low. Doc chalked it up to heredity," Hanrahan said, scanning the pages of his notebook.

There were Cubs on first and third with one out. Grace hit into a double play. The Cockers groaned and the little boy in the next booth turned to look at the crazy old men.

"So, Father Murph," Lieberman said just before sipping his coffee, "what do we have?"

"None of Rozier's neighbors remember a handyman coming to their door. None of them has hired a handyman in months. Checked three blocks square. Should have brought my raincoat."

"So either our thief was checking out the Rozier place . . ." said Lieberman.

"Or there was no thief," said Hanrahan, looking up. "I don't like our recent widower. His grief is fake."

Lieberman nodded. Hanrahan was a world-class griever.

"That doesn't make him a killer, Father Murph."

The Cockers chattered. The family at the next table left. Harry Carey said there were two more chances for the Cubs, and a trio of truck drivers came in and sat at the counter.

"Man can be happy his wife is dead, or at least not unhappy, and not be responsible for her death," said Lieberman. "And he has a hell of an alibi."

"Could have hired somebody," Hanrahan countered.

"Could have. Could also be telling the truth."

"Could. You don't like him either, do you?"

"No," Lieberman confessed, wondering if he could start his diet tomorrow. What could one day hurt? One last bash before the long starvation. Who ever died of a hot dog? But he knew he wouldn't do it. There was no tempering for Abe Lieberman, never had been. He could give it up, but he couldn't settle for just a little.

"So?"

"You take Harvey," Lieberman said. "Find out if he inherits from his wife, if he's been cheating on her, or if she's been cheating on him. Check the alibi. Be careful. Our Harvey is an important man."

"I'll make it quick and quiet, call in a few favors," said Hanrahan as Manuel returned and placed a huge sandwich in front of him. The pickle on the plate shone green and new.

"I'll go for the thief," said Lieberman, looking at the toasted bagel in front of him and the small carton of red jelly. "Rozier asked me the names of five perps in the mug books. Says none of them was the would-be handyman. For a man who claims to remember faces the way Charlton Heston remembers Shakespeare, his asking for the names strikes me as—"

"Odd," said Hanrahan, opening his mouth to attempt to encompass the enormity of the sandwich in his hands.

Lieberman took a bite of his toasted bagel and stood up.

"I'll call Evidence and the coroner," he said. "Enjoy your sandwich."

The phone was through the door to the kitchen, right

next to the men's room. He made his calls, took notes holding the receiver tucked under his chin, asked questions, and hung up. When he got back to the booth, the Cubs had miraculously tied the game, the truck drivers' mouths were stuffed, and the Alter Cockers were laughing. The new Cocker, Morris Becker, was doing something with his face that may have been smiling.

Hanrahan had, thanks to God, finished his sandwich and pickle.

"What do we have?" he asked.

"Puzzles," said Lieberman.

"I don't like puzzles," said Hanrahan, sucking at something in his teeth.

"Doing the autopsy now," he said. "I talked to Reasoner. He said he'd wring my neck if I let anybody know before Brice told us officially, but it looks like Dana Rozier was killed by multiple stab wounds in her arms, legs, back, stomach, chest, and face. No sexual assault with or without the weapon."

"So where's the puzzle?"

"They found ipecac in her stomach," he said. "The stuff that makes you throw up fast."

"I know. So, she accidentally ate something that she thought was—" Hanrahan began, but Lieberman was shaking his head.

"Our friend Dr. Reasoner says it doesn't look like there was anything in her stomach, that she hadn't eaten for at least six to eight hours. Still preliminary, but . . ." Lieberman shrugged.

"I'll see if there's any ipecac at the Rozier house," said Hanrahan, working on his coffee as the Pirates scored one in the top of the ninth to go back out ahead by a run. "What else?"

"Remember the mark in the blood, rectangle, about six inches by a foot and a half?"

"Yeah, looked like the blood had flowed around it."

"Evidence said they didn't take anything from the room. Didn't move anything," said Lieberman.

"Maybe," Hanrahan tried, "the killer put something

down when he killed Mrs. Rozier. Then when he was done, he picked it up and ran."

"Nope," said Lieberman, working on his now-cold bagel. "Whatever was there was a good seven or eight feet from the body. It took awhile for the blood to get to there."

"How long?" Hanrahan asked.

"Who knows? Two, maybe three minutes. Man kills a woman in panic when he's caught in a burglary and then waits a minute or goes back to looking for candlesticks?"

"Not likely, unless he's a real hard-core addict," Hanrahan answered. "But it's still possible, Rabbi."

"Most self-respecting thieves who hadn't planned the crime would get the hell out of there as fast as they could. So I ask you, Father Murphy, what made that shape in the blood and where is it?"

"Cubs win! Cubs win!" Harry Carey shouted. "Holy cow."

"I'll be looking for our mysterious object," said Hanrahan, "but . . ."

"It's probably nothing. I know. Last puzzler. Fingerprints found match Rozier, Franklin, his wife, the dead woman. Footprints in the blood also check for Rozier, Franklin, and his wife plus two others, one with sneakers."

"Two burglars?" said Hanrahan.

"We'll ask when we find one of them, Father Murphy," said Lieberman.

Manuel came to the table bearing two side orders of potato pancakes with sour cream.

"Compliments of the boys," he said, nodding at the Cockers' table. "In honor of the Cubs' victory."

Lieberman looked at the Cockers, who raised their seltzer, chocolate phosphates, and coffee in a toast to the Cubs.

Were latkes on Doc Berry's hit list? Absolutely not, Lieberman decided. At least not till I ask Doc Berry. And with that he dug in.

When he left to drive Bill Hanrahan home fifteen minutes later, Maish had still not returned.

* * *

The hardest thing for Harvey Rozier to do was keep from working. Playing the role of grieving husband was proving to be the most difficult part of murdering his wife. He sat in the living room trying to look overwhelmed while Betty Franklin, who had relieved her husband, fielded endless calls from business associates, Harvey's secretary, near and distant relatives, and the media.

The bloody toolbox the thief had left was locked inside Harvey's second safe in the garage. The safe was behind the tool cabinet and looked as old as the house, which had been built in the 1920s.

He had to find that thief, the witness to his crime. He had his name, George Patniks or Eupatniaks. He would check the city and suburban directories and, if necessary, ask a friend in the phone company to see if the man had an unlisted number. No, Harvey decided. He couldn't do that. No more than he could simply have someone in City Hall call the thief's parole officer or check the files to find the man's address. He couldn't have anyone who could trace him to the thief, particularly if Harvey had to kill him.

If the man were reasonable, Harvey told himself, he might consider threatening him with revelation as the murderer, complete with the man's bloody toolbox as evidence. He might. But Harvey doubted it.

Tonight, when he was alone in his room, he would check the directories and hope that the man was listed. If he wasn't, the job would be that much harder.

There were no parking spaces on the street in front of his house, not even the one by the fire hydrant. A van with a CLERGY sign on the pulled-down visor was illegally parked there.

Art Hellyer was joyfully announcing the next string of oldies on the radio as Lieberman turned the corner on Birchwood and drove around the back into the alley.

The rain had stopped, and there was a heavy, cold Chicago spring chill as Lieberman got out of the car, found the right key on his chain, and opened the garage. The garage door had ceased subservient cooperation more than a decade ago. It grew more reluctant with each opening. Weary from Chicago heat, cold, and rain, it simply wanted to be left alone. Normally Lieberman honored that wish, but there were a few nights, like tonight, when it was either park two or three blocks away or try to wake the dying door. Lieberman struggled, pulled, heard the impatient humming of his car engine behind him. Trying to lift with his knees and protect his back, Lieberman coaxed and pampered as the door reluctantly began to slide upward with a rusty squeal.

No more, Lieberman decided. He would not park in the garage again. He would fill the garage with junk from the closets. It was either that or fix the door, a challenge he did not even give serious consideration.

It was late, later than he liked, a little after eight. A little talk with the kids before they went to bed, some contentious banter with his daughter, something to eat—but what?—and then to the bedroom with Bess if he didn't get a call.

Abe opened the porch door, crossed the few feet to the back door. He heard the loud, confident baritone voice the instant he opened the door. The voice sounded familiar. Abe kicked off his shoes and placed them on the sheet of newspaper laid out next to the door. The aroma of cooking brisket filled the room. I'm undone, Lieberman thought.

"No doubt, none whatsoever," the man's voice pontificated from beyond the closed kitchen door.

"Well . . ." Bess answered.

Abe had crossed the kitchen, opened the door, and met his wife's eyes. She and the man were seated at the dining room table.

Bess was five years younger than Abe Lieberman. On a bad day she looked fifteen years younger. On a good day she looked like his daughter. She was Abe's height, dark, and slender. Not a classic beauty but a Lady, a lady with a capital L. She wore her curly dark hair short and she had the most beautiful and distinctive soft voice Lieberman had ever heard. Bess's father had been a butcher on the South Side, but Bess, now the president of Temple Mir Shavot, carried herself as if she had come from generations of successful bankers.

"Oh, Abe," she said looking up at him. "I was hoping you'd be home. You know Rabbi Nathanson?"

There was something in Bess's voice that made it clear she needed support or rescue.

Rabbi Ira Nathanson of Temple B'nai Shalom, south of Devon, rose and held out his right hand. In his left hand was an envelope. Rabbi Nathanson was a tall man, four or five years younger than Lieberman. His shoulders sagged and his dark face and heavily bagged eyes had given him the nickname among the children of Rabbi Camel. The rabbi was wearing a dark suit and tie and a grave look.

"We've met," Lieberman said, taking the rabbi's large hand in a firm shake. "Three years ago. Member of your congregation, Isadore Green. Missing person."

"Ah," said Rabbi Nathanson, standing back and shaking his head with his hands folded in front of him. "Never found. May the Lord have taken him to his bosom."

"Amen," said Abe, looking at Bess for guidance. It had been Lieberman's conclusion that Isadore Green had simply run away and was probably alive and well in Gallup, New Mexico, or some point even farther west.

Bess shrugged.

"Coffee, Abe?" she said. "More coffee, Rabbi?"

"Later," said Lieberman, joining them at the table. "Where are Lisa and the kids?"

"Todd took the kids to a movie, *Die Hard 3* or *4* or something. Lisa's working late."

Alone at last, Lieberman thought, loosening his tie and looking at Rabbi Nathanson, who had nodded to indicate that more coffee would be welcome. Bess moved toward the kitchen.

Nathanson opened his mouth to speak but Abe stopped him with, "I'll be right back," and headed for his and Bess's bedroom.

In the bedroom, as he did whenever he came home, Lieberman opened the drawer of the night table on his side of the bed, using the key he always wore around his neck.

He put his .38 and holster into the drawer, closed it, and locked it with the key, checking to be sure the drawer was indeed locked. Then he returned to the dining room and the waiting visitor.

"Let me explain," said the rabbi, folding his hands on the table, "as I did with your wife, who, I would like to add, is doing a monumental job as president of Mir Shavot during the move to the new synagogue. Monumental."

"Thank you," said Lieberman, also folding his hands on the table.

Bess came back with the coffee pot and poured more in the rabbi's cup. The rabbi nodded in appreciation and returned his steady eyes to Abe's face.

"Rabbi Wass, your rabbi, indicated in conversation that you were planning to move, to be closer to the new synagogue site," the rabbi said in a near whisper, as if this were very confidential information.

" 'Planning' is a little strong, Rov," Lieberman said, looking at Bess across the table. She shrugged to indicate she had nothing to do with spreading such a rumor.

"Well," Nathanson said, "it may come as no surprise to you that congregation B'nai Shalom is seriously considering a move to this neighborhood to serve the older Jewish community, those who cannot easily move to the north with you, and to serve the young Russian immigrants who are coming to this area in ever-growing numbers."

It was not Lieberman's place or desire to contradict the rabbi, at least not till the man came to the point. Rabbi Camel had the reputation of delivering meandering sermons in which the point came late and was usually missed by the congregation. The older Jews in Lieberman's neighborhood were dying off, moving in with their children in the suburbs, or lounging in Florida high-rises if they could afford it. Some Russian immigrants were moving in, but the vast majority of those moving in were Asians and Indians and a few upwardly mobile Hispanics. The neighborhood change was the primary reason Temple Mir Shavot was moving thirty blocks north.

"We may build," Nathanson said, holding up one hand

and then the other, "or we may buy a suitable edifice. It is unfortunate that the building you are abandoning has been sold to Chinese Christians."

"Korean," Bess corrected.

The Koreans, Lieberman knew, had made the best offer and Bess, Rabbi Wass, and the building committee had decided that the Korean Baptist Church and its leader Reverend Kim Park were conservative, honorable, and far better than the only other offer that they had received, from Kenehay Exporters, a group that Lieberman labeled after one phone call as being engaged in "dubious" enterprises.

"My wife . . ." Nathanson went on.

Lieberman pointedly looked at his watch. Bess frowned at her husband's manners and Rabbi Nathanson seemed not to have noticed. He was launched. There was no stopping him.

"My wife, Leah, and I have sold our house. The children, Larry and Rachel, are off at college. Rachel is at Brandeis. Larry is finishing dental school, University of California."

"That's wonderful," said Bess. "Isn't it, Abe?"

"A blessing," said Abe.

"Expensive," sighed the rabbi. "But for your children . . ."

"You make sacrifices," Bess concluded.

"So you sold your house," Lieberman prompted.

"Sold our house, where we had loved, nurtured, and raised a family," the rabbi went on. "Sold and moved into a condominium."

"That's nice," said Bess.

"We hate it," Rabbi Nathanson said forlornly. "No history, no character. We hung our paintings—you've heard of the priceless painting of the Torah we have, the one done by Hammasha of Jerusalem?"

He looked at Bess and Lieberman, who nodded slightly, neither knowing about this famous artwork.

"Well, it does not hang well in the apartment," he said sadly. "A cold museum no matter what effort my poor Leah puts into it. But this house . . ." He looked around the dining room and into the living room. "This house has a history, a family, the aura, if you will, of Jewish culture."

Lieberman nodded knowingly, sure that the aura was in part a failure to invest in new furniture for more than fifteen years plus the brisket simmering in the kitchen.

"Thank you," said Bess. "You sure you don't want coffee, Abe?"

"Later," Lieberman said, now fascinated by the apparently pointless but elegantly presented ramblings of the rabbi.

"In short, I wish to buy your house. I'm sure you will be reasonable," said the rabbi, pausing for a response.

"I don't think we're seriously considering selling quite yet," Lieberman said.

"Abe . . ." Bess said softly.

"Well, maybe," Lieberman conceded.

"Good," Rabbi Nathanson said leaning forward, ready for business. "A price?"

"One hundred and seventy-five thousand," said Bess.

Rabbi Nathanson sat back to consider this.

"No realtor, six and a half percent saved," said the rabbi. "One hundred and sixty-two thousand and five hundred dollars."

"We could consider that," Bess said, looking at Lieberman, encouraging him with her eyes not to destroy this opportunity.

"We'll think about it," said Lieberman.

The rabbi put down the envelope in his hand, pulled out a fountain pen, and began writing.

"I will now give you a check for one thousand dollars," he said. "Earnest money. Good faith money to be applied to the purchase price. In return, you sign this document stating that you will sell to no one else for six months."

"I don't think . . ." Lieberman began, but Rabbi Nathanson was hunched over his envelope and the checkbook he had conjured from his pocket. He was lost in words and dollars.

"There," he said, handing check and envelope to Lieberman, who looked at them and turned the envelope over. It was a mailer from a Honda dealer on Western Avenue. Lieberman handed check and envelope to Bess.

"No offense, Rabbi," Lieberman said, "but I think we should think this over and talk to our lawyer before we sign anything."

Rabbi Nathanson nodded, all knowing, and said, "Fine, but I want you to keep the check, hold it, deposit it. I want this perfect house. I want to bring my wife to see it. How is tomorrow night for you?"

The Liebermans exchanged looks and Bess, holding the check in her hand, said, "Fine."

"Seven?" asked the rabbi.

"Seven," agreed Bess as the tall rabbi took the envelope back and signed it.

"There. You have my check. You have my signature."

The rabbi rose. So did the Liebermans. They shook hands and walked their guest to the front door. On the way he scanned the walls, ceiling, and furniture with interest.

"The lighting fixtures," he said at the door. "They stay with the house?"

"Sure," said Lieberman.

"Good," the rabbi said. "Good. Tomorrow. Seven."

He hurried down the steps to the CLERGY car parked in front of the fire hydrant. Lieberman closed the door and looked at his wife.

"He's nuts," said Lieberman.

"Unorthodox," Bess said, handing her husband the rabbi's check.

"Reform," Lieberman amended, looking at the check. "And he has the handwriting of an ax murderer."

They were moving back toward the kitchen now, where Bess would feed him and grill him about his visit to Dr. Berry.

"Handwriting analysis is not your specialty," Bess said, taking his hand.

"It doesn't take an expert to see frenzy, the zeal of a true believer," Lieberman said.

"We have a nice house," Bess said, moving to the kitchen table.

"Then we should stay in it," Lieberman said, sitting.

The table was already set for one.

"We agreed to think about selling," Bess said. "And fate brought us Rabbi Nathanson. The house is too big for two."

"Lisa . . ." he tried, but she was ready.

"Will be moving out soon and we'll have the heat, air-conditioning, repairs, cleaning . . ."

"We'll think about it. Don't cash the check. Give Denenberg a call and ask him what he makes of it. What time do you have to leave?"

"Leave?" she said.

"Table set for one. You're wearing a suit with pearls and perfume at eight o'clock. The great detective put the clues together. Building committee?" Lieberman asked.

"Fund-raising committee," Bess answered. "You'll have some time alone, to take it easy."

She came around the table and kissed him. She tasted sweet and Lieberman wondered if they had time to . . .

"Al and Sophie Bloombach are picking me up in—," she said with a smile, knowing what was on his mind, "—about ten minutes."

Lieberman sighed.

"You'll have to be satisfied with a thin slice of brisket, potatoes, and salad till I get back, if you're still feeling frisky and awake."

"No brisket," Lieberman said as his wife moved to the oven. The smell from the oven was irresistible. "After tonight."

Bess turned to him.

"What did the doctor tell you?"

Abe tore a piece of challah from the half loaf on the table in front of him.

"His name is Berry, Jacob Berry, Jewish. Just came to the city from Indiana or Michigan. He's in his mid-thirties, divorced, loves baseball, has no sense of humor, and is easy to push around. Perfect for Lisa. I thought we might invite him—"

"Abe," Bess said patiently, hands on her hips.

"High cholesterol, liver enzymes still high but manageable, migraines under control, back holding up, arthritis as well as can be expected. End of report. Nothing new."

"We have to watch your food, Abe. You promised me you'd live to be a hundred and nine."

"My love, if I am going to make it to one hundred and nine, the Lord will have to be very generous and he will need massive sacrifice from me. No meats, no milk products, watch the fat and cholesterol, lots of vegetables and fruits ... in short, a potentially long life of extreme deprivation."

"We'll find ways to make it taste good and good for you," she said. "Brisket is made. Indulge yourself, Abraham. One piece."

"I am persuaded," he said, and she brought the brisket to the table.

Bill Hanrahan did not want to go home, did not want to return to the house haunted now by the memory of his wife, Maureen, and children, in addition to Frankie Kraylaw, whom he had shot and killed just inside the front door. No one and nothing waited for him but a layer of distorted dreams covered by a layer of sour memories.

Hanrahan ate his sweet-and-sour pork. He had not quite mastered chopsticks, but he was reasonably comfortable with them. There were two other customers in the Black Moon Restaurant, an older couple probably from one of the high-rises across Sheridan Road. The old couple had paid and were waiting for Iris Chen to bring their change.

Through the restaurant window across the street, Hanrahan could see the entrance to one of the high-rises, the one in which a prostitute named Estralda Valdez had been murdered because William Michael Hanrahan was drunk while on duty. He had met Iris while using the Black Moon as a vantage point for watching the entrance to the high-rise. He was drunk when he met Iris, but she still agreed to go out with him. And their relationship had meandered now for over a year.

Iris gave the old couple their change and moved over to take a seat across from Hanrahan.

She was, he thought, lovely. He knew she was older than she looked, that she was older than he, but she looked young and solid and good, and being with her made him feel calm.

"We were talking about Laio Woo," Hanrahan said, picking up a small, perfect square of pork.

"I remember," said Iris. She was dressed in a blue silk dress that was decidedly Oriental, the uniform of the Black Moon. "He does know my family. He . . . my father borrowed money from him to open this restaurant. Mr. Woo has demanded nothing for this but prompt and reasonable payment of the very low-interest loan."

"He never made any passes at you, nothing like that?"

"No," Iris said with a smile. "Mr. Woo is a very old man."

"Old men are not dead men," Hanrahan said, making headway on his rice.

"I have seen Mr. Woo maybe six, seven times," she said. "He has always been polite and distant. If Mr. Woo wanted women, he could have as many pretty young girls as he wants."

"Don't underestimate yourself," Hanrahan said, reaching over to take her hand.

It was smooth, delicate.

"Mr. Woo comes from a poor family in China," Iris said, looking down at the white tablecloth. "My father believes that he wants simply to be respected, acknowledged as the leader of the Chinese community. My father believes that Mr. Woo thrives on adulation and longs for respect. My father believes that Mr. Woo will never forget what he was as a child and fears to be as an adult. My father says Mr. Woo can be very dangerous."

"When are you going to marry me, Iris?"

"When would you like?"

"End of the month," he said.

Iris pulled her hand out of his and sat back.

"Because Mr. Woo has said you should stop seeing me, you suddenly want to marry?"

The kitchen door opened and Iris's frail father stood in the doorway in his apron.

"Not to spite Woo," Hanrahan said, though he knew there was a bit of that in his decision too. "I've had enough of being alone and I'm more at peace with myself when I'm with you than I've ever been in my life."

Iris's father didn't move. Though Hanrahan had lowered his voice, he was sure the old man could hear him.

"I think my father agrees with Mr. Woo," Iris said. "I think my father asked Mr. Woo to talk to you."

Hanrahan looked at the somber old man in the doorway.

"Don't be angry with my father," she said, touching Hanrahan's hand.

"I'm not," said Hanrahan. "I'd like to be angry at somebody, but I'm not. I'm clearly not Chinese. I'm a cop with a drinking problem and I keep strange hours, mope around, and disappear for days. He and Mr. Woo make a lot of sense. Will you marry me? I can quit and we can pack up and be out of Chicago in two weeks."

Mr. Chen turned and went silently back into the Black Moon kitchen.

"And we escape," she said, stroking the back of his hand.

"Something like that," he agreed.

"I will think about it," she said.

"I'd like to talk to your father," he said.

"Not a good time, William," she said, sliding out of the booth and glancing toward the kitchen.

He dropped a ten-dollar bill on the table but Iris reached over, picked it up, and handed it back to him.

"I'd rather pay," he said.

"Not in my house," she said, leaning over to kiss him.

The position was awkward as he sat but she did it gracefully.

"Can we go somewhere?" he said. "Maybe back to my house? We've got a lot to talk about."

"Not tonight," she said, touching his cheek. "I must be with my father."

"I understand," said Hanrahan. "Or at least I accept that I don't understand."

He was out of the booth now and reluctant to leave.

"Call me tomorrow, William," Iris said gently.

And Hanrahan made his way to the door and out onto Sheridan Road.

He stood for a moment and looked toward his car. He should go back to the house, maybe watch some television, do some paperwork. Sit sober and alone. He couldn't, not yet, not this early. He could go to a movie but there was nothing he wanted to see and he was sure he would fall asleep and snore.

Hanrahan decided instead to pay a late-evening visit to Harvey Rozier.

"I say shit, we forget it, man," said Albert Davis, slouching back in his chair at the rear of the McDonald's on South Shore Drive. "Why we wanna go all the way back uptown so far from our own turf? Somethin' go two farts in the wind and where we gonna run? Up on an el platform and wait for the Englewood B train with the cops all over us?"

"We go in. Take what we want. We tape him up, shove him in a closet, something, and we go out, maybe catch a cab," Iago Simms said, his left eye almost closed as he chewed on a double cheese.

It was a little after nine at night. The place was crowded, mostly with young people, all black, mostly making noise and laughing. Lonny, Iago, and Dalbert in a back booth had to talk above the noise. They didn't care who heard them.

"You out you fuckin' mind, man?" Dalbert said with irritation, looking at Lonny Wayne for support or direction. None came. Lonny looked cool, sat straight up, touched the brim of his White Sox cap, and went on eating the fish sandwich stuffed with french fries. "What cab driver gonna pick up us? No white or nigger driver, that's for sure. And what we gonna do? Walk the streets with all kindsa shit, drugs what all, looking for a Chink driver?"

"We get wheels," Lonny said, looking over Dalbert's head at a girl who sat with two other girls and a boy. The girl was young, maybe fourteen, fifteen, chocolate skin, maybe Haitian, maybe Jamaican. He'd seen her around, thought maybe she was new in the neighborhood. She was sexy and wore a tight sweater she kept hitching up to be sure her big boobs showed.

"Shit," said Dalbert.

"Garages back on thirty-seventh, you know?" asked Lonny, catching the girl's eyes. She met his look for an instant, then turned and went back to her conversation. Lonny Wayne needed money to get a pretty girl like that. Hell, Lonny needed money to get any girl except Railroad Monique, and she was just a crazy bitch with all kinds of teeth missing.

"Sure," said Iago.

Dalbert shrugged.

"Bag Man Reno keeps his wheels in one of those little garages, big old Chrysler, couple years old maybe," Lonny said. "Bag Man's out of town. Heard it from my old man, heard him tell Jackson the barber."

"You sayin' what I think you sayin'?" Dalbert asked incredulously. "You wanna steal Bag Man Reno's car? Man, someone see us they tell for sure and we get our dicks cut off like that Bobbitt guy on TV."

"We be borrowin' the car," Iago squealed, his half-sagging face pushed toward Dalbert. "Jus' borrowin', and we bring it right back. Ain't that the way, Lonny?"

"That's the way," Lonny said.

"When?" Dalbert said, resigned and reaching for a french fry as a sign that his rebellion was over.

"We take the wheels tonight," said Lonny. "Park 'em over in the hospital lot. Get it tomorrow, maybe three, four. Get the doc and wait till night to put Bag Man's car back."

"Ain't easy," said Dalbert, simply making conversation now.

"Ain't nothin' easy this world," said Iago.

Lonny caught the girl's eye again, unsure of whether she was interested. Maybe she was just fascinated by the lightning bolt scar through his right eyebrow. Like Juanita. Just wanted to touch it and put her tongue in the space between his teeth. Juanita one dead junkie now. She had been a crazy bitch.

"What the fuck?" Lonny said and stood up.

"Where we goin'?" asked Iago.

"Watch my ass," said Lonny, walking toward the three girls and the guy. He knew when he got close that he was right about them. They were talking funny, like French.

"Hi," he said.

All four looked up at him. They were all young, but the boy was a little older and his eyes said, I'm on somethin' heavy, don't mess with me. Lonny smiled, space between his teeth, looking only at the pretty little girl. Lord, she had great big white teeth.

"I'm Lonny Wayne," he said, taking off his hat. The girls giggled. "And who might you all be?"

"People who want they should be left alone," the young man said angrily.

"Be polite," one of the girls said. She wasn't as pretty or as big as the girl Lonny wanted, but she had a big red mouth. "I'm Martine. And this is Adrienne and Denise." So her name was Denise. "And this is Andre."

"Count Andre," the young man said. "Count of after you mess with me you better count your fingers. Now you introduced, how about you go back to your table before you're counting fingers?"

"How about you talk nice? I ain't been saying nothin' wrong. Have I, ladies?" Lonny said with a grin.

"No," all three girls said.

A screaming and laughing heavy girl ran past, bumping into Lonny, who almost fell over the table into Denise's lap.

"You got a phone number?" he said.

The girl named Martine laughed.

"Hey, get the fuck out of here," said the count. "Don't be messin' with my cousin."

Lonny ignored him. The pretty Denise, who looked just as good up close as from across the room, nodded.

"Can't give it to you," she said. Great voice—and that accent. "My mamma doesn't want me to go out with boys yet. Says I'm too young."

"Not from where I'm standing," Lonny said.

The other two girls at the table whispered to each other and the count stood up, reaching for his pocket. He never got that far. Dalbert had the young man's wrist and Iago stood with his back to the table showing something to the angry young man, something that made the count ease up.

"No hard feelins here, my man," Lonny said. "What say I pay for a round of burgers all round. And then we sit talkin', me and my friends, with you all for awhile?"

The count had no choice. He sat flanked now by Dalbert and Iago.

"What you got?" Lonny said, standing up and fishing four dollars from his pocket. Dalbert coughed up two bucks and some change and Iago found three dollars, mostly in change.

"Be right back," Lonny said and began making his way through the crowd to the counter.

No doubt now. He needed money.

And he knew where he was going to get it.

Unwelcome Visitors

When the doorbell rang, Abe had just settled in his bath with his book of crossword puzzles. On the floor in reserve, if he so desired, lay last Sunday's *Tribune Magazine*.

It couldn't be Todd with the kids. Barry had a key. Unless he forgot or lost it.

Lieberman got out of the tub, dried himself quickly, and put on his blue terry cloth robe. The doorbell rang insistently. He slipped on his battered slippers, a Hanukkah gift from Maish and Yetta, and hurried into the hall, across the dining and living rooms to the front door. The bell was ringing as he opened the door and found himself facing Rabbi Nathanson and a small woman. A fine rain was falling and the woman was wincing as if each drop was an acid assault.

"See," said the Camel triumphantly, "I told you. He's here. Lieberman, we have to talk."

With that, the rabbi and the woman, who looked a bit like a sparrow, pushed past Abe Lieberman. Abe had no choice but to close the door and turn to his guests, who were already choosing their places at the dining room table.

"This is my wife, Leah," said Rabbi Nathanson, holding out his long arm in the woman's direction.

She smiled politely at Lieberman.

"Rabbi, this is a bad time," said Lieberman, still standing and rapidly coming to the conclusion that anytime the Camel appeared at his house was going to be a bad time.

"A minute, a minute only," the rabbi said, removing the yarmulke from his head so that he could run a broad palm over his moist hair. "Even the Lord gave Joshua a minute.

Even the great Rabbi Eleazar could always spare a minute for anyone who sought his counsel or his company."

The rabbi's coat was partly open now and Lieberman could see that he was in his pajamas.

"I don't want to be rude, Mrs. Nathanson," Lieberman said, avoiding the open chair near the table. "But I've had a long day and as you can see . . . ," he said, looking down at his robe and slippers.

"You are a policeman," said Nathanson with a knowing nod of his head. "The stories you must have. The things you must have seen. We live in a world of chaos, in a time of violence. We need, our people need, salvation and comfort in the word of our God."

"Amen," Mrs. Nathanson said dutifully.

"Amen," said Lieberman. "Now, Rabbi, if you—"

"I wanted Leah to see this house, this perfect house, and I wanted to urge you to cash the check I gave you. Every day we delay is a day further from the realization of a new home, a much-needed home, for my congregation and my family."

"Rabbi," Lieberman said. "I have to talk to my lawyer."

"Why?" asked the rabbi, looking at his wife, who had no answer. "I'll pay your price. My wife will have no other house."

Mrs. Nathanson was, for the first time, looking around the room, at the walls, into the semidark living room, toward the closed door of the kitchen.

The sound of a key in the front door gave Rabbi Nathanson no pause.

"To be homeless is a curse of our people, Lieberman. Delay creates anxiety. Anxiety results in neglect of one's duties and places a burden on those we love and who depend upon us."

Lieberman's grandchildren, Barry, approaching thirteen, and Melisa, eight, stepped in with their father, Todd Cresswell, behind them.

Mrs. Nathanson smiled at the trio. The rabbi didn't seem to notice their arrival.

"Lieberman, who knows?" he said intently, leaning

toward Abe, who stood dripping before him. "Who knows how much time God has given us for the work we are to do on this troubled earth? Do we delay over the obstacles of civilization heaped high with distrust?"

"Rabbi, Mrs. Nathanson," said Lieberman, "this is my son-in-law Todd and my grandchildren, Barry and Melisa."

"We saw *Beethoven's Second*," said Melisa, who, Lieberman thought, looked exactly like her mother at the age of eight. Serious, studious, suspicious.

Todd, tall, with a handsome, lopsided face, cornstalk-straight hair, and rimless glasses, nodded at the Nathansons. Barry, who closely resembled his father, looked at Abe for an explanation of the presence of the night visitor in pajamas.

"Rabbi Nathanson and his wife are interested in buying the house," Abe explained.

Todd, whose hair was a rain-scattered mess, nodded and said, "Lisa's . . . ?" Todd began looking toward the kitchen.

"Working late," Lieberman said.

Todd nodded.

"Do not pain a hungry heart," Rabbi Nathanson went on. "And do not anger a man who is in want. Do not increase the troubles of a mind that is incensed. And do not put off giving to a man who is in need. Make yourself beloved in the congregation, and bow your head to a great personage. Listen to what a poor man has to say and give him a peaceful and gentle answer."

"Rescue a man who is being wronged from the hand of the wrongdoer, and do not be fainthearted about giving your judgment," Todd said, looking at Lieberman.

Rabbi Nathanson turned in his chair to face the challenging presence of Todd Cresswell.

"The Wisdom of Sirach from the Apocrypha," explained Todd. "The rabbi left out a line."

"Todd's a classics professor at Northwestern," Lieberman explained. "Cresswell's his name. Greek tragedy's his game."

"The Apocrypha was written in Greek," Todd explained to Barry as if the assembled adults all knew this already.

"It's part of the Greek version of the original Jewish Bible. The parts not included in the final, accepted version of the Hebrew Bible are called the Apocrypha, the hidden or secret books."

"Your father was a rabbi?" asked Rabbi Nathanson.

"My father was a Methodist minister in Dayton, Ohio," said Todd.

Rabbi Nathanson, truly perplexed, looked to Lieberman for explanation and, finding none, said, "Lieberman, I must press you for a decision."

"Saint Bernards drool a lot. Even in movies. Can I have some ice cream?" Melisa said.

"Yes," said Lieberman.

"I'll get some too," said Barry.

Melisa and Barry hugged their father and hurried into the kitchen, closing the door behind them.

Todd made no move to leave, so Lieberman said, "Todd and I have some things to discuss. So . . ."

"Open ye the gates, that the righteous nation that keepeth faithfulness may enter in," said Rabbi Nathanson.

"Isaiah," said Todd. "Houses clear in their right are given children in all loveliness."

"Numbers?" tried an obviously challenged Rabbi Nathanson.

"Aeschylus," said Todd. *"Agamemnon."*

"Rov," said Lieberman, "I think you've been outquoted."

"Ira, let's go home," Mrs. Nathanson said, rising and moving around the table to touch the arm of her husband, who was desperately searching his memory for a quote—Maimonides, Eleazar, the Talmud, Franklin Roosevelt. Nothing came. He rose, and his wife reached up to button his coat.

"We'll talk tomorrow," Rabbi Nathanson said as his wife led him to the door.

Lieberman followed, moving past Todd. He opened the door and ushered the Nathansons out into the drizzle. The tall, gangly rabbi stepped down the concrete steps, and his wife turned to whisper quickly to Lieberman.

"I'm so sorry. Ira has been . . . distraught."

"Leah," the rabbi called, moving down the narrow cement path toward the street.

Mrs. Nathanson turned and hurried to join her husband as gentle thunder echoed far away. Lieberman closed the door and turned back to Todd Cresswell, who was still facing the dining room.

"I was in the bath, Todd," Lieberman said, moving into the dining room to face his son-in-law.

"I'm sorry," Todd said. "Abe, I'm . . . I'm agreeing to the divorce."

Lieberman shook his head. Beyond the closed kitchen door Barry and Melisa were arguing about something.

"This doesn't surprise me," Lieberman said.

"I didn't think it would. By nature all men are shy and . . ."

"No," Lieberman said, holding up both hands. "No Sophocles."

"I was going to quote Euripides."

"No Greeks," said Lieberman. "I'm having a long night. You want to marry . . . ?"

"Faye," Todd said softly, glancing at the kitchen door. "Yes."

Lieberman nodded. He had met Faye Cunningham once when Todd had picked up the kids for a weekend. She was, as Lieberman remembered, a good-looking dark woman with an honest smile and large teeth. She was definitely older than Todd, and though Lieberman had been prepared to dislike her, he had found her pleasant and obviously in love with Todd.

"Abe, Lisa and I are too much alike," Todd said.

"I know," Abe agreed. "It's a curse. It doesn't work if you're too much alike or too different from each other. The answer is somewhere in between."

"You're joking," said Todd, adjusting his glasses. "I'm serious."

"I'm dripping. You're serious."

The kitchen door flew open.

Barry was holding a plastic bottle of Hershey's chocolate syrup over his head. Melisa was trying to reach it.

"Mom says she shouldn't have chocolate at night," Barry said. "It makes her wild and abstract."

"Grandpa," Melisa pleaded. "The ice cream needs chocolate sauce. It's vanilla."

"A little chocolate sauce, Barry," Lieberman said. "Vanilla ice cream without chocolate sauce is a tragedy."

"OK," said Barry, handing his sister the bottle. "It's your call, but if she goes nuts, you tell Mom."

"I'll tell your mother," Lieberman agreed and the two children disappeared into the kitchen.

"They acted as if I were already gone," said Todd, adjusting his glasses.

"I like Faye," said Lieberman.

"Lisa and I are both tragedy," said Todd. "You understand? Faye is comedy."

"I understand," said Lieberman.

Lieberman had admitted it to no one but himself that Todd was, indeed, better off without Lisa. Though she was his own daughter, there was an air of martyred despair and seriousness about her that definitely came from generations lost in antiquity and the farmlands north of Kiev from which both Lieberman's and Bess's grandparents had come.

"Then you'll . . . ?"

"Talk to Lisa, yes," Lieberman agreed.

"And then I'll talk to her. I promise," said Todd, allowing himself to be ushered toward the door.

"I believe you," said Lieberman, opening the front door.

"Remember, Abe, it was Lisa who wanted some freedom, who walked out with the kids."

"I absolve you, Todd. Go forth into the world and live a life of goodwill and self-fulfillment."

"Abe, don't—" he began, opening the front door.

"I'm sorry, Todd. I'm tired. I'm hungry for a dozen Ritz crackers covered with chopped liver. I want to shave in a hot tub and do a crossword puzzle. I want 'The Henry Morgan Show' to return to radio. I want a new stomach, new knees, and everything to be the way it was in 1958. Is that too much to ask?"

"It can't be," said Todd.

"I know. Good night. I'll talk to Lisa."

Todd nodded, adjusted his glasses, plunged his hands into the pockets of his denim jacket, and hurried into the night. It was raining harder now.

He found them at the kitchen table working on white ice-cream mountains covered with syrupy chocolate. Abe Lieberman longed to join them.

"Can I count on you two to clean up and go to bed reasonably clean?"

"Can we watch television for an hour?" Melisa said, her nose dotted with chocolate. "I have no trouble waking up in the morning. You know that."

Barry looked at the ceiling, making it clear that he would not join this debate.

"One hour," Lieberman agreed. "You both watch the same thing. Upstairs. In bed. No fights. You hear your mother and the lights go out before she catches you. Deal?"

"Deal," Melisa said.

"She'll tell," said Barry.

"I won't," Melisa insisted, jabbing her spoon into the softening mound of ice cream and chocolate.

"We'll see," said Barry, looking exactly like his father.

"I'm getting back in my bath. Good night," said Lieberman.

"Don't see *Beethoven's Second*, Grandpa," Melisa said as he went out the door. "It sucks."

There were lights on in the Rozier house—not a lot of lights, but enough to suggest that the grieving Harvey Rozier was not swooning in bed a few minutes before ten.

There were no private security men on the door.

Hanrahan knew why he didn't like Rozier. The man was arrogant and his grief a fraud. That didn't make him guilty of killing his wife or hiring someone to do it. Many unlikable people are innocent just as many a murderer is a decent individual. Still, Bill Hanrahan did not like Harvey Rozier.

He rang the bell. A chime echoed. Pause. He rang again and heard footsteps coming down the stairs. Then the door opened and Harvey Rozier, barefoot, in pale jeans and a red Chicago Bulls sweatshirt, was glaring at the policeman at his door.

"You didn't ask who I was before you opened the door," Hanrahan said.

"You're right," Rozier said with irritation.

"Don't want to take chances," said Hanrahan.

"I'll be more careful," said Rozier.

"You know who I am?"

"One of the policemen who came this morning. Detective Lieberman's partner. I'm sorry, I don't remember your—"

"Hanrahan, Detective William Hanrahan. Mind if I come in?"

"What's happened?" asked Rozier.

"A few questions. I'll be fast."

"Who is it, Harvey?" came a woman's voice from inside the house.

"A policeman, Betty," Rozier answered, and then, to Hanrahan, "The Franklins won't let me stay here alone."

"Good friends to have," Hanrahan said, stepping past Rozier into the hallway.

Mrs. Franklin, her white hair cut in a perfect cap and wearing an appropriate black dress, stepped out of the living room just to the left of the hall.

"This is Detective Hanrahan, Betty," Rozier said. "He has some questions. You've met Mr. Franklin. This is his wife."

The woman was a bookend match for the tall lawyer Hanrahan and Lieberman had dealt with that morning. Tall, distant, and annoyed.

"I'll call Ken," she said, moving to the phone on an antique table against the wall.

"Let Ken get some rest," Rozier said. "I'm sure I can answer Detective Hanrahan's questions without my attorney."

"Couldn't this have waited till the morning?" Mrs. Franklin asked. "Harvey's been through—"

"I'll be quick," said Hanrahan. "I thought you'd be

pleased that we're putting in late hours trying to find the person who murdered your wife."

Rozier nodded, brushed his hair back, and motioned toward the living room. Hanrahan followed, with Mrs. Franklin behind him to be sure he didn't pocket some valued bric-a-brac.

The Rozier living room was right out of one of those movies about French kings two hundred years ago. Dark wood, fading but light fabric with twining vines and flowers. Sideboards and sofas with spindly legs, and paintings on the wall of dogs and deep woods.

Neither Rozier nor Mrs. Franklin sat.

"Ipecac," said Hanrahan. "You have ipecac in the house?"

"Ipa . . . ?" Rozier began, looking puzzled.

"The stuff you use to induce vomiting when you've accidentally swallowed something poisonous," explained Hanrahan.

Rozier should have known that. They weren't dealing with some esoteric drug here.

"Yes, of course," Rozier said, suddenly understanding. "I'm sorry. A little surprised. I don't think we have any ipecac. Why . . . ?"

"Your wife had more than a trace of ipecac in her stomach."

"Why on earth would Dana . . . ?" Betty Franklin said, clenching her hands.

"That makes no sense," Rozier said, sitting on one of the old French chairs. "Why would she take ipecac?"

"Maybe she didn't," said Hanrahan. "Maybe someone gave it to her."

"What?" cried Betty Franklin. "Why would anyone give Dana something to make her throw up?"

"Who knows?" Hanrahan said, his eyes never leaving Rozier. "Maybe someone wanted her sick and at home last night. Maybe she knew the killer who planned to murder her."

"That's insane," said Betty Franklin. "Why would anyone want to murder Dana?"

"Somebody did," said Harvey Rozier. "Go on, Mr. Hanrahan."

"Mind if I check around, see if we turn this ipecac up?"

"Can't it wait till tomorrow?" asked Rozier. "Or Betty and I can look and let you know—"

Something in Hanrahan's eyes stopped Rozier cold with the knowledge that the policeman suspected him. But there was no reason to suspect him. It was a technique. That was all. Everyone's guilty of something. Keep the witnesses, suspects, and victims on edge. Harvey had employed the same technique with clients and business enemies. When Lieberman had chiseled at his alibi this morning, it was no more than Harvey had expected. It took only an occasional look at the ten o'clock news to know that the spouse who survived a murder was the prime suspect and very often the murderer. It was a situation he had anticipated and prepared for.

"I see," said Rozier.

"See what?" demanded Betty Franklin, moving to a table and removing a cigarette from a dark enameled box.

"I'm a suspect," said Harvey, smiling up at her.

Now that she had something to do with her hands, Betty Franklin was a bit more calm.

"I'm calling Ken," she said, moving toward an old-fashioned phone on an end table near Rozier.

"No, Betty," he said, moving quickly to her side and putting his hand over the phone to stop her from calling her husband. "Detective Hanrahan is just doing his job. He suspects me. He suspects Ken. He suspects you."

"Ken? Me?"

Mrs. Franklin sat in a chair across from Rozier, played with the cigarette in her fingers, and looked up.

"That is absurd," she said. "We were at the recital. You saw me. You saw Ken. And we saw you."

"You saw each other the entire night?" Hanrahan said. "I'm just trying to eliminate even the slightest suspicion, you understand."

"Why not check with the ushers or Mrs. Gabriel?" Rozier asked. "Someone must have seen . . ."

"We checked," said Hanrahan. "No one noticed if any of you left the concert hall."

"We glanced at Harvey frequently," Mrs. Franklin said with indignation. "We knew he was concerned about Dana and we wanted to be ready to leave if Harvey wished to do so."

"And I will vouch for the Franklins," said Harvey, "but I think Detective Hanrahan is considering the possibility of an accomplice actually killing Dana."

"Maybe two accomplices," said Hanrahan. "There were two sets of unidentified footprints in Mrs. Rozier's blood. One set led to the broken dining room window and down the driveway. The other set led to the back door and disappeared. Strange. The killers go in different directions and one seems to have taken off his shoes at the back door."

There was little that could be called distraught in Rozier. In fact, Hanrahan felt that the man was reassessing him, considering what the proper response should be. There wasn't a type Hanrahan had not seen in his more than twenty years as a Chicago cop. A pause. Rozier decided.

"Please, go look for the ipecac," he said, rising, his voice quivering just slightly. "And please be quick. And please go out and find the person or persons who killed Dana. And please do not come ringing my doorbell at night without calling first."

"Can't you see the man is in agony?" Betty Franklin said to the policeman.

"Yes, ma'am," Bill Hanrahan said, but he felt that he was watching a man pretending to be in agony. "Now, if we can . . . ?"

"I'll go with you," Rozier said, meeting Hanrahan's eyes and making it clear that no underpaid policeman was going to wander unattended through his house. "Betty, please stay here."

Betty Franklin had placed the cigarette in her mouth but hadn't lit it. Rozier touched her shoulder to reassure her and handed her a lighter, which she accepted with a nervous nod.

Less than three minutes later Hanrahan had found the

small bottle in Dana Rozier's dressing table. Hanrahan took a zippered sandwich bag from his pocket and slipped it around the bottle, easing it inside the plastic without touching the bottle.

"You don't mind if I take this, do you?"

"No," said Rozier, arms folded, watching. "Why would Dana keep something like that?"

Hanrahan pocketed the bottle and shrugged.

"Bulimia, fear of being poisoned—who knows? I've heard the damnedest reasons for the damnedest things."

"Are we finished?" Rozier asked.

"We are," said Hanrahan, looking around the tastefully antiqued bedroom. "Just one more question."

"Ask your question, Detective. And then go find Dana's killer."

"You didn't find a box, something about this wide and this long, on the floor in the kitchen before the police got here?" Hanrahan said, moving his hands to show the approximate size of the object that had been outlined in Dana Rozier's blood. "I mean after your wife died and before the police came."

The puzzled look came almost instantly but not quite fast enough. Hanrahan was sure he saw a tic of something, maybe fear, in the face of Harvey Rozier.

"No," he said. "Why?"

Hanrahan shrugged and didn't answer. He turned away from Rozier, looked around the room, and then walked slowly out with Rozier behind him.

At the bottom of the stairs, Mrs. Franklin was standing in the hallway, nervously smoking as she waited.

"Well?" she asked.

"We found the ipecac," said Harvey Rozier, coming down the stairs. "Did you know that Dana had this? Or why?"

"No," said Betty Franklin.

"Sorry to have bothered you," Hanrahan said, meeting Rozier's eyes and extending a hand.

They both knew that Hanrahan was not in the least sorry.

They shook like gentlemen and the policeman let himself out.

"I'm going to ask Kenneth to complain about that man," Betty Franklin said, putting out her cigarette and glaring at the door. "You should be getting rest, not harassment."

"He's doing his job," said Rozier, stepping toward her.

"He could do it more politely," she said. "They can't find Dana's killer so they intrude on you. I think you've had enough for one day. Harvey, you should go to bed."

"I agree," he said with a yawn, "but on one condition."

"Yes?"

"That you come to bed with me," he said.

Betty Franklin moved into his arms and opened her mouth to his kiss.

Hanrahan drove and listened to the radio. Late-night meaningless talk. All-night meaningless talk. A voice in the night as he drove. He couldn't bring himself to turn on the radio at home, but in the car he would listen to almost any voice in the night.

It was still early, not much past eleven, and there were thoughts, feelings that didn't want to be named, that wanted to swim in the numb of amber Scotch.

Ten minutes later he stood in front of the Blue Parrot Lounge on Broadway, no more than five blocks from the Rogers Park Station. Hanrahan didn't know where the sweat began and the rain took over. He stood in the near cover of the overhang before the entrance, a soothing neon-red-and-gold rinse on his skin, the smell of ribs from Wesley's across the street and in front of him, beyond the familiar door, the sound of rhythm vibrating without melody from the jukebox.

Bill Hanrahan rubbed his eyes. The neighborhood stank and was getting worse, but only one ignorant hold-up man had made the mistake of stepping through the double doors and pulling a third-rate piece from his pocket. That was four years ago. It had taken the gunman only a second look to realize that he had screwed up royally. The place was stacked with cops, all of them looking like cops, a few of them in open-collared uniforms. By then it was too late and the gunman, whose name was Robert Jefferson Davis Jointz, had taken three bullets in the leg and one in the right chest, taking out his lung. Jointz was now breathing heavy and doing time in Stateville.

Memories of the Blue Parrot, its smell, its soothing brown lights with promises of Silver Bullets over the bar, returned fast and sharp. Hanrahan pushed open the doors and stepped inside.

The music sounded no better inside, some raspy-voiced wailer from the sixties. Elvis, the Everly Brothers, Creedence Clearwater, and early Johnny Cash would be along in a minute or an hour.

In the booth near the jukebox, Applegate and Acardo, Black and White, were arguing. Applegate's finger was in his partner's face. Both held partly filled glasses protectively.

Ernie Cadwell was at the bar talking to a woman from Vice whose name Hanrahan couldn't remember.

"William," a voice called over the whant-waink-thud of the guitar and drum from the glowing jukebox.

Nestor Briggs was in the booth beyond the arguing Acardo and Applegate. Nestor was holding up a stein of beer and waving at Hanrahan. Hanrahan made his way past three full tables of people, most of whom were cops, almost all of whom he recognized. Nothing had changed.

Nestor was alone. Hanrahan slid in across from him and a woman with enormous breasts, frizzy blond hair, and the serious look of a priestess appeared almost immediately.

"What'll it be tonight, Irish?" Ramona asked.

As if he hadn't been gone for almost half a year. She hadn't noticed the six months that had seemed a life sentence to hard time.

Hanrahan looked at the table.

"You want a beer, William?" asked Nestor Briggs, leaning toward him. "A beer ain't drinking."

Hanrahan nodded and Ramona drifted toward the bar.

"Reminds me of an old Irish story," Hanrahan said, looking around the familiar room, the photographs of dead cops on the wall, the autographed photograph of Jim McMahon on the wall over the jukebox, and the other autographed photo of old Bill Nicholson over the bar, complete with the old Cubs uniform and a loopy grin.

"It seems that Doyle Murphy left the town of Galway when he was a poor boy of seventeen determined to make his fortune in Australia and return to Galway in triumph. The years passed and Doyle worked his way up from dock hand to shore boss to union steward to labor to minister of labor and the boards of four major shipping companies. He was rich and, in the right circles in Sydney and Perth, famous."

"A success story," said Nestor, rubbing his sweating bald brow. "Here's to him."

Nestor raised his glass of Scotch and melted rocks and toasted Doyle Murphy of Galway.

"More to the story," Hanrahan said as the pause between jukebox records was filled with Applegate at the next table bellowing, ". . . and I say he was holding two full Ks if he had an ounce." Then Elvis, familiar, sad, belted, "It's now or never."

"Doyle took the boat home and then a train, and on a summer's night almost fifty years after he had left Galway," said Hanrahan, nodding to Ramona, who had returned to place a full, cool stein before him, "he stepped off the train, set down his suitcase, and looked down the platform, where an old man was moving slowly toward him. When the old man was half a dozen feet from Doyle, Doyle recognized him as his boyhood friend Conan Frazier. 'Doyle,' says Conan, 'is that you?' 'It is,' said Doyle, standing tall in his handmade silk suit. 'Well,' said Conan, 'I see you got your suitcase. Where are you off to then?' "

Nestor Briggs took his drink from his lips and looked puzzled. Hanrahan looked down at his beer and put his big hands around it.

"I think I'm back in Galway," he said.

"I heard you were riding the wagon, William," Briggs said.

"Well . . . I tell you, Nestor, it's hard to go home to an

empty house. It's hard to be a saint. It's hard to lie to yourself and not believe your lies."

". . . our love won't wait," Elvis belted.

"I know," said Briggs, shoving an almost empty blue bowl of nachos in front of Hanrahan. "Truth is," he went on, lowering his voice and biting his lower lip, "I live right around the corner, you know, and the only thing waiting up for me is my dog. You know why I'm whispering? You a Catholic?"

"Yeah," said Hanrahan.

"I hate the fucking dog, hate him," Nestor Briggs confessed. "I pretend I like him and maybe some ways I do, but he's old and he farts and I have to walk him and feed him and be home with him. When my wife died I figured I needed companionship. Everyone thought I should have a dog. Old Nestor should have a dog. So I got a dog. Now I hate to go home and take care of him. You want a dog?"

"You make it sound tempting, Nestor my friend, but I'm going to have to control my boyish urge and say no thanks."

"Ever change your mind, you know where to find me. I throw in his bed, blanket, all the dog food I've got stored. He has his shots. He . . . shit, who'm I kiddin'. I couldn't give him away. I'd feel . . ."

Nestor didn't know how he'd feel. He finished his drink, sucked his teeth, and looked at the empty glass. Then he stood up.

"I'm going home," he said, fumbling for his wallet.

"Want me to walk you?" asked Hanrahan.

"On our first date?" Nestor said with a slurred laugh. "Never."

"I'll cover the drink," said Hanrahan. "Me and Doyle Murphy."

"Doyle . . . ? The guy from Galway? Whatever happened to him?" asked Briggs, looking up at Bill Nicholson over the bar.

"He went back to Australia," said Hanrahan, rising. He fished a ten-dollar bill from his wallet and dropped it on the table. "I'm walking you home, first date or no, and I promise not to kiss you or get in your jockey shorts."

Nestor Briggs shrugged and allowed himself to be led toward the door.

"Hanrahan," Applegate shouted. "You're Irish. You'll know this one. When you get Briggs home, come back and we'll settle this."

Johnny Cash was walking the line with his eyes wide open. The stein of Coors on tap bubbled on the table, untouched, as the doors of the Blue Parrot closed behind Hanrahan and the weaving Nestor Briggs.

The rain had slowed to near mist.

Somewhere nearby a lonely dog was waiting.

When Mothers Dream

"You know, Gregor," Wanda Skutnik said to her son as she sat in her favorite chair and tried to talk over Jenny Jones. "Those things on the things."

She held out her hand and moved it about as if she had developed a regional palsy.

"I don't know, Ma," George said.

"Oh," Wanda said in exasperation, trying to find the right words. "The ones my sister gave me when she came in . . . nineteen and eighty-two."

"The coasters? Little round things with flowers on them?"

Wanda nodded, relieved.

"You gave them to Mr. and Mrs. Karawan for Christmas, before I went back . . . Look, Ma, I want to talk about Seattle again."

"I know," Wanda said, sitting up, eyes not leaving the television screen, where Jenny was arguing with a fat, bearded man who had a wife and a mistress who used to be a man.

"Look, Ma."

She held up her hand. "I know what I was trying to think of before the little round things. A mouse."

"Ma, we don't have any mice."

"Not the animals," she said, shaking her head at her son's denseness. "The ones on the typewriters with the screens."

"You mean the mouse on the computer?" asked George.

"Yes," she said, relieved. "If you have more than one mouse, is it mouses or mice?"

"Why would anyone have more?"

"If you sold them you would have more," she said patiently. "If you were the person at the computer store who sold them and you had to order more."

"I don't know," said George. "I don't know what you'd call them."

George Patniks was defeated.

He hadn't slept well last night. Dreams, fears, and shadows. He had gotten up a little after four, taken a shower, gotten on some reasonably clean sweats, and gone back to the painting. By a few minutes before eight, when he heard his mother's feet shuffling across the floor above him, George finished the painting. He stepped back and examined it, waiting for the release he wanted.

The woman was vivid now, her face pleading with horror, and the robed figure above her, knife in hand, was looking out of the canvas as if he had discovered the painter. Harvey Rozier's face was as vivid as his wife's. The white-white of the kitchen in the painting contrasted with the deep pool of dark blood on the terrazzo floor. Things were reflected in the blood, dark, grinning things only suggested by light and shadow. And in the midst of the blood sat George's toolbox, mundane, out of place, inappropriate for the horror depicted.

It was probably the best work George Patniks had ever done, but he'd never be able to show it. He didn't want to show it. He wanted to take the image from his memory and banish it to the canvas.

Should he have jumped out and gone for Rozier, tried to save the woman? He had been surprised, hypnotized, as if watching a horror movie suddenly thrown up on his ceiling in the middle of the night. Even if he had jumped out, George had reasoned as he looked at his painting, the woman was nearly dead already, wasn't she? And the floor was covered with blood. George would have slipped and Rozier would have been all over him. George shuddered. That picture was clear and sudden. He hoped he didn't have to paint it. Wait, Rozier had a knife and Rozier was in better shape and outweighed George. George had done all he could do. He had saved himself.

But the phone. George had cut the phone line. Dana Rozier had gone for the phone, her last chance, and had gotten nothing. Rozier had been through the door and had attacked her within seconds, but would those seconds on the phone been enough for her to call 911 and simply say, "My husband's killing me"?

"You should take a shower, Gregor," Wanda said.

"I already took one," he answered, looking at himself and realizing that he was, once again, covered in paint. "Ma, I want to pack today and go to Seattle for that art fair. You don't want to come, OK. I'll call Tommy. He and Sissy can look in on you, maybe stay awhile."

The doorbell rang.

George's hands clutched the arms of the chair, knuckles and hands white under dabs of blue and red paint.

"The mistress is better looking than the wife," Wanda said, looking at the television screen and clearly not hearing the doorbell. "And she ain't even a woman. I see that all the time."

The doorbell rang again.

This time she heard it.

"Gregor, the door. It's ringing," she said, looking at her son. "Gregor, are you OK? Get the door. It's probably Mrs. Vivlachki or someone."

The doorbell rang again and George got up. His mother was right. He couldn't go through this every time the doorbell rang. Rozier couldn't have found him this quickly. Rozier would probably never find him, especially if he moved to Seattle for awhile. He'd have to tell his latest parole officer, but . . .

The doorbell rang once more.

George shuffled past his mother and into the little hallway with the tiny faded fringe rug. George took a deep breath and opened the door.

The rain had stopped but the dark skies suggested that it was only a temporary halt.

Before him stood a man about George's size, maybe

sixty-five or older, curly white hair and a little white mustache. The man looked weary and bored, and George knew with certainty that the man was a cop.

"Gregor Eupatniaks?" asked Lieberman.

"Yes, but my legal name is George, George Patniks."

Lieberman was wearing an open raincoat over his brown jacket and a tie he had gotten for his birthday from Barry and Melisa. The tie depicted little brown World War I airplanes circling purple clouds against a dark blue background.

"Name's Lieberman. I'm a detective with the Clark Street Station in Rogers Park. I think you know the neighborhood."

Lieberman took out his wallet and showed his ID card.

"Yes," said George.

"Can I come in?" asked Lieberman.

"My mother's watching TV. She gets upset cops come around. You know?"

"We can get in my car, go for a coffee," offered Lieberman reasonably.

"OK, sure," Patniks said. "Let me just tell my mother."

Lieberman nodded and stepped into the house.

"I hear you're a painter," Lieberman said.

"Yeah."

"I like painting. Things that look real. Is that the way you paint or do you do things that don't look like anything?"

"My paintings look like things," George said nervously.

"I'd like to see them," said Lieberman.

This was a nightmare. Not the one George had anticipated, but a nightmare. You go on a job and suddenly a man is murdering his wife. You hear the doorbell ring and there's a cop wanting to look at the painting you did of the guy who killed his wife. Nightmare. George's legs went weak.

"Maybe sometime. I'll tell my mother," he said.

From the hallway Lieberman watched the man move to a heavy woman planted in front of a Sony television set.

George leaned over and said, "I'm going out for a half hour or so. This man wants to talk to me."

Wanda Skutnik turned heavily in her chair without turning her neck. The chair creaked. Jenny Jones was shouting, "Wait a minute. Wait a minute."

"OK if I change my shirt, pants—just take a minute?" George asked.

Lieberman nodded and George hurried for the door that led down to his room.

"You're a police," Wanda said.

"Yes."

"You are old for police," she observed.

"I just look old," Lieberman said. "The job does it to you."

"Mrs. Maniaks's nephew, Stan. He was a policeman. You knew him?"

"Don't think so," said Lieberman.

"He took money from the stores on Division. And then he wasn't a policeman."

The woman nodded and Lieberman asked, "Is there a way to the street from George's room?"

"Door," she said. "Stand by the window over there and you can see it, but George isn't going to run away."

Lieberman moved to the window and looked out.

A commercial came on. A woman was wild with enthusiasm for the Home Shopping Network.

"You can get some good buys on Home Shopping," Wanda said. "I got a clock that looks like a soldier, alarm clock. Screams at you, 'Get up. Rise and shine.' "

"Sounds cute," said Lieberman.

"What?"

"Sounds cute," Lieberman repeated loudly.

"Gave it to one of my sons, Tommy, for last Christmas. You think they have Home Shopping in Seattle?"

"Probably," said Lieberman.

The woman sighed deeply.

"I don't think I want to go to Seattle," she said. "My legs, it's far. Who needs travel at my age?"

"You've been thinking about visiting Seattle?" he said.

"Gregor, he's got this *vishmite*, this thing about going to an art show, fair, something in Seattle. Gregor is an artist, a painter. He had ribbons and one time . . ."

Her voice trailed off and then she sighed and asked, "What did Gregor do this time?"

Below him through the thin floor, Lieberman could hear George Patniks shuffling around, moving things. What could he be moving?

"I don't know that he did anything," Lieberman said. "I just need some information from him. Night before last. You remember if he was home?"

"Night before . . ." Wanda Skutnik turned to the television set for inspiration. "Not last night, but . . . He was home. All night."

"Good," Lieberman said with a smile.

With George Patniks having his own entrance and a hard-of-hearing mother, the woman's information didn't mean much. Lieberman checked his watch. Almost two minutes. He was about to go after Patniks when he heard the sound of footsteps coming up from below. George, now wearing jeans and a neatly ironed white shirt, came through the door. There were still dabs of paint on his forehead and hands.

"Wear a jacket," Wanda said as George moved toward Lieberman.

"I will, Ma," he said, opening a closet and pulling out a zippered blue jacket. "I'll be right back."

"Pleasure to meet you, ma'am," Lieberman said.

Of the five men whom Harvey Rozier had asked about as he looked through the tapes and books of mug shots, one was dead, one was in the Federal Security Prison in Marion, another had moved to a farm in Tennessee. Lieberman had found one of the two remaining men, Sandoval "Sandy" Borchers, in his apartment on Claremont. Borchers, a born-again Christian, told Lieberman that he worked nights, including the night of the murder, at the Toddle House on Howard Street. A call to the night manager, who had to be awakened by his wife, confirmed that Borchers had been working with the manager and another worker all night, no time away from the restaurant from eight at night till four the next morning. That left George Patniks, who was proving to be a promising prospect.

"You want to know why I'm here?" Lieberman asked as they got into the car parked in front of the house.

"Sure," said George with a shrug.

"You seemed curiously uncurious," said Lieberman. "You want a coffee?"

George shrugged again. Lieberman reached down, removed two Dunkin' Donuts coffees from a bag, and handed one to George.

"Thanks," he said.

The coffee was warm but no longer hot. The two men drank and watched the thin rain that had returned in the last few seconds. Across the street someone peeked through first-floor curtains. All of the houses on the block were small, wooden, and old with little front yards enclosed by low fences.

"You know a man named Rozier?" Lieberman asked.

"No," George answered, looking straight out the window at nothing and shaking his head. "Knew a con named Rozell. That be the guy?"

"No," said Lieberman, pausing to take a sip of tepid coffee. "Your entire life you're sure you've never run into someone named Rozier?"

"Not that I recall. You meet a lot of people."

"You want to know why I'm asking?"

George shrugged to show that he didn't care.

"Your mother says you're planning a trip to Seattle."

"Thinkin' about it."

"What's in Seattle?"

"Art fair. Chance to sell some of my paintings. I do pretty good at paintings. Learned it inside."

Lieberman looked over at the person watching them through the parted curtains across the street.

"Everyone here know you're a con?"

"Most everybody. We've got no neighborhood newspaper. Lot of people couldn't read it if we did," said George.

"What's the name of this fair in Seattle?" asked

114

Lieberman. "My wife's an art lover. Maybe we can fly up for a day or two, see the sights, taste the wares, go to an art show."

A young woman holding a coat over her head with one hand and the hand of a small white-haired boy with the other came out of the house next door. The rain was a little harder now, more than a drizzle. The woman hurried, dragging the boy along and across the street in front of Lieberman's car. The boy's eyes met the detective's. Then mother and child were gone.

"Cute kid," said Lieberman.

"Peter, Peter Wascaboinik," said George, resisting the urge to rub his hands together or play with his ring.

"The art fair, George. We were talking about an art fair in Seattle," said Lieberman. "You were going to give me the name of the fair and maybe a name and number of someone running it."

"Off the top?" George asked, still not meeting Lieberman's eyes. "Who remembers?"

"You got it written down. We can go look," Lieberman said reasonably.

George laughed, afraid his voice would break and give him away.

"What is all this?" he said, finally turning to meet the detective's waiting eyes. "OK, there is no art fair in Seattle. I just want to get away from here for a week or so, pick up a woman. I've got a little saved. Seattle, that's just something I told my mother. And what difference it make if I shack up with a whore in the Loop or go to Seattle? What's it prove one way or the other? What you want from me?"

All said with a combination of pain, indignation, and self-righteousness.

Lieberman kept looking at George Patniks and drinking his coffee.

George blinked first, turned his head forward, hit the dashboard and said, "Damn."

"Woman was found dead night before last," said Lieberman. "Murdered. Mutilated. Good-looking lady before it happened."

"Sorry to hear it," George said, sounding genuinely sorry.

"Her husband said a man came around early part of last week looking for handyman jobs. Man fits your description. You a handyman now, George?"

"No," he said.

"You mind being in a lineup?"

"I never went to no one's house saying I was a handyman. This is nuts."

"Then you won't mind a lineup."

George shrugged and said, "I'm busy."

"An hour. No more. Maybe a little less. You know I can get the papers and have you uptown by this afternoon. You have something to be afraid of, George?"

"Oh, Jesus," George groaned.

"I beg your pardon," said Lieberman. "I'm not asking you to confess to murder, George. I'm just asking you to stand in a lineup. You've done it before. Lots of times."

"When you want to do it?"

"Now's not bad. Maybe an hour or so from now so I can call our witness," said Lieberman.

"I never met this guy Rozier," George said. "Honest to God. Hand to my heart."

"Rozier? Who said the husband's name is Rozier?"

"Come on, Liebowitz—"

"Lieberman."

"Come on, Lieberman," George said wearily. "You ask me do I know a guy named Rozier. Then you tell me there's a dead woman and her husband talked to a handyman who maybe looked a little like me."

"Seems logical," Lieberman said, pursing his lips. "Shall we proceed to the lineup?"

"I gotta tell Ma," George said.

Cool rainy spring morning. George Patniks was sweating. Lieberman decided to make him sweat a little more.

"Good," he said, opening the door. "We can take a few minutes and look at some of your paintings."

"You've got no warrant," said George as Lieberman got out.

"Patrons of the arts don't need warrants, George. They get invited in by starving middle-aged painters. You got something in your room you don't want me to see?"

"No," said George with mustered indignity.

"A quick look," Lieberman said softly, getting out of the car. "What can it hurt?"

"Nothing," said George, letting himself be guided back to the house by the policeman.

They went back into the house to the cry of Wanda Skutnik calling, "Take the shoes off or wipe the feet good."

Both George and Abe Lieberman wiped their feet on the little runner in the hall.

"Gonna show Mr. Lieberman some of my work. Then we got to go out for awhile."

Wanda turned to watch the two men as they headed for the door beyond which was the stairway leading to George's room.

"What have you done this time, Gregor?"

"Nothing, Ma. Nothing. Watch your show."

"Montel has a stupid show today," she answered. "Policeman, what did my son do this time? Who did he rob?"

"I'll have him back in less than three hours," answered Lieberman, following George through the door.

"That's an answer to my question?" she shouted. "Trapped in my own house. No one tells me anything. Are you hungry? You want some roast beef and potato salad?"

Lieberman followed Patniks down the narrow wooden steps.

George's room was a mess. Paints and paintings, palettes and newspapers, an unmade bed, piles of magazines. Lieberman wondered what George had been moving when he heard him through the floor less than ten minutes earlier.

"Nice work," said Lieberman, holding up a painting of a woman behind what looked like the counter of an all-night diner. The woman looked sad. There were no customers for whatever she was selling.

"Thanks," George said.

"What are you working on now? Don't artists have easels, something?"

"I'm not working on anything now."

"Then how'd you get covered with paint?"

"Mixing, looking for colors," explained George weakly. "I'm in the sketch stage. Pencil. Here, I'll show you."

George found a pad and opened it, flapping through pages of dark men and darker shadows.

"Illuminating," said Lieberman.

"Thanks," said George. "Can we go now?"

Lieberman looked around the room and nodded. Above them the television cackled.

"Let's go out the back," George said.

On the way across town to the station, Lieberman called Harvey Rozier and asked him to come to the station, said it was definitely important, that he had a possible line on the so-called handyman.

"Ken and I will be right there, and Lieberman, I think it only right that I tell you I've issued an official protest about the conduct of your partner who came to my house last night and treated me as if I were the prime suspect in my wife's murder."

"He is willful," said Lieberman.

"Is that sarcasm, Officer?" the quivering voice of Ken Franklin said, obviously from an extension.

"The truth," said Lieberman. "I'll see you at the station in an hour. Mr. Rozier knows the way."

When he hung up, Lieberman turned to George Patniks. There was no doubt that the man at his side was perspiring like a kid with a bad case of pneumonia.

Ken Franklin turned to Harvey Rozier and said, "They're more than a bit high-handed, these policemen, but they do seem to be giving full attention to the case. Are you all right, Harv?"

Harvey Rozier stood pale and sweating in his University of Illinois T-shirt and shorts, a towel around his neck. He had just finished forty minutes at 5.0 on the treadmill in the basement and now he stood in his office study wondering if there were some way he could get out of this. He had no choice but to agree immediately to Lieberman's request that he come and identify the man they had found. In all likelihood it wouldn't be Patniks. He had decided to wait till the immediate furor over Dana's death had faded before he located and contacted Patniks. But now this. And what about the mistakes he had made? Harvey Rozier had been confident that he could carry this off, but he had never murdered anyone before and he certainly couldn't have anticipated that a burglar would be a witness to the crime.

The ipecac, the ipecac—that was the mistake. He should have said Dana kept it around because she had a fear of food poisoning. Perhaps he could remember this casually, even refer to some time when she got sick and they were nowhere near a doctor. Nassau last year.

"Harv?" Ken Franklin said with concern, moving to the younger man. "Are you all right?"

"Under the circumstances, fine," said Rozier, giving his lawyer the faint smile of the victim who is doing his best to bear up under his grief.

Franklin smiled sympathetically and said, "You'd better take a shower and get dressed."

Rozier nodded and left the room.

There was something else he had not considered in this. He had a nearly perfect alibi, and he had told no one of his plan for murder, but what he hadn't counted on was the police coming up with the idea that he might have hired someone to murder Dana. He wasn't sure that this was their line of reasoning, but it made more than a little sense.

He stripped in the bathroom, leaving his clothes on the floor for the housekeeper to pick up. He wondered for an instant how Dana paid the woman. He would have to ask.

Harvey ran the water as hot as he could tolerate and it pelted him into thought and revived his confidence. Ken would stick by him, as would Betty, who, given her age, was in great condition and much better in bed than he would have imagined when he started to move on her almost six months ago.

Confidence, he told himself. There's no way they can get you on this, no way. Give you a hard time? Yes. But that would be it, and Ken, providing his health held up, would stand in front of Harv and take the worst of it.

Harvey had purposely not varied his work routine in any way before the murder. Even though he knew he would not be coming in for weeks, he had made appointments, set up meetings, made promises. This morning he had called Alan Gibson and told him to carry on as best he could and Alan had dutifully told him not to worry.

He had left to Betty the job of contacting Dana's relatives and booking them into the Hyatt. Betty had told them that Harvey was too distraught to see anyone yet.

Ten minutes after he stepped into the shower Harvey was dressed and downstairs. Ken was standing in the front hallway waiting, a newspaper in his hand.

"You haven't looked at the newspapers, have you?" Franklin asked.

"You asked me not to."

"Television?"

"Not the news."

"Good. The invasion of privacy will go on for a week or two and start to fade. No reason for you to be reminded of . . ."

"Thanks, Ken. I don't know what I'd do without you and Betty."

"We'll take my car," Ken said. "It's in the driveway."

Harvey nodded gratefully.

The crowd of curious observers was gone and the murder of Dana Rozier, while not forgotten by the press, was yesterday's news, particularly since it was clear that Harvey Rozier would not respond to questions.

Harvey climbed into Franklin's Lincoln Town Car, closed the door, and tried to think of how he should handle the situation if, by some stroke of luck or Harvey's error, they had found Patniks.

Confrontations

Hanrahan was late. When Lieberman called him and told him to get to the station, Bill Hanrahan had just finished shaving and putting on his clothes. His tie was still open, but that could wait till he got to the front door.

He had pulled in the *Tribune*, read the Rozier story at the top of page two, and found that Captain Kearney had been quoted to the effect that there were several good leads, that the crime was one of the most wanton and savage he had ever worked on, and that Harvey Rozier was bearing up remarkably well.

Hanrahan was on his second cup of coffee. He had eight more in the coffee maker. He hadn't bought a new, smaller machine when Maureen left him, and it was automatic with him to grind the beans and fill the machine with ten cups. He'd reheat it in the microwave when he got home at night and dump what was left when he went to bed. Caffeine didn't keep Hanrahan awake at nights. Sometimes his shattered knees ached and the need for the prescription pills that eased the pain woke him in a cold sweat, but usually it was thoughts, thoughts of Maureen, Iris, the boys. He fought the rage and bitterness and the lure of the bottle, and each day he won, but it took a lot out of him. And he needed coffee.

Someone knocked at the front door. Hanrahan put down the newspaper and, cup of coffee in hand, went to the door, opened it, and found himself looking at three Oriental men. All were dressed in dark suits. The one in the middle looked like one of those dogs with the wrinkled faces. The ancient man wore thick glasses and carried a cane, simple, bamboo.

"Mr. Hanrahan," the old man said. "May I have but a brief word with you?"

Hanrahan looked at the two younger men. They looked fit and smart, probably knew some martial arts crap that looked good in the movies. No, he decided quickly, they had too much class for that, and besides, the bigger one to the old man's left was definitely carrying a weapon under his jacket. He didn't need martial arts.

"I've only got a few minutes," Hanrahan said, stepping back to let them in.

"That is all we shall take," said the old man, nodding as he and the other two stepped into Hanrahan's living room.

Hanrahan closed the door as the old man looked around the room.

"Modest and clean," the old man said with approval.

"Glad you like it," said Hanrahan. "Coffee's in the kitchen. We can sit."

"You know who I am?" asked the old man, following Hanrahan to the kitchen.

"Wouldn't take much of a detective to figure it out," Hanrahan said, holding the door open so the trio could enter the kitchen.

Hanrahan motioned the men to the table. Laio Woo closed his eyes and nodded at the other two men to sit. They did and so did he.

"Do you take anything in your coffee?"

"Black for all of us," said Woo, placing his cane on the kitchen table.

"I could get you tea," said Hanrahan.

"I do not care for tea," said Woo.

All very polite so far, thought Hanrahan, serving his visitors coffee and sitting down in the chair left open for him. Hanrahan put his coffee cup down and neatly folded the newspaper.

"You are a fastidious housekeeper," said Woo. "That is admirable."

"As I said, I'm glad you approve," said Hanrahan, checking his watch.

The four men drank for a minute or more without speaking and then Woo placed his cup on the table, folded his hands, and looked at Hanrahan.

"You know why I am here," he said.

"To keep me from marrying Iris Chen," Hanrahan said.

"Mr. Chen, Iris's father, informs me that in spite of my associate's call to you, you have pressed your suit with Miss Chen and asked that she marry you."

"That I did," said Hanrahan, a phrase his father used frequently.

Maybe the formality of his guest moved Bill Hanrahan to the Irish formality of his father. He could clearly hear the accepted voice of County Kildare, and it rested inside him like a Cheshire cat, a silent voice with no face.

"Please understand," said Woo, leaning forward. "Miss Chen would be ostracized from her community. Her father would be shamed. You are Caucasian, divorced, an alcoholic. Am I being too blunt?"

"It cuts through the bullshit," said Hanrahan with a smile.

"Yes," said Woo pensively.

"Is that it?" Hanrahan said, looking at all three men and standing up. "I've got to get to work."

His eyes met the old man's and held.

"This marriage might be good for you. Iris Chen is a good woman, but it would not be good for her. What she would gain from you could not possibly compensate for what she would lose. You do not look like a selfish man. If you would, please tell me with honesty if you believe me wrong."

"Oh, Lord," Hanrahan said with a sigh. "No, much as I'd dearly like to throw the three of you out and break your cane over my knee, you're right. I'll do some more thinking about it."

"You have been a lonely man," said Woo. "Do not sacrifice Iris Chen to your fear of being alone. I say this because I know what it is like to be alone."

"I appreciate that," said Hanrahan.

Woo, with the help of his cane, stood up, and the other two men joined him.

"You have a look of failed expectation," said Woo, facing Hanrahan. "Did you expect me to threaten you, try to bribe you?"

"Maybe."

"Would that have had any effect?"

"No," said Hanrahan. "You handled it just right."

Woo extended his hand and Bill Hanrahan took it. It was a hand of wrinkled skin and thin bones. The policeman was careful with it.

"You need not show us out," said Woo, heading for the kitchen door with his men.

"But I wish to," said Hanrahan, leading the way.

The three visitors made a move with their heads that might have been a bow and left without a word.

"Quite a show," Hanrahan said aloud when the door was shut behind them.

A lot of polite reason, he thought, and a hidden weapon or two. Hanrahan wasn't afraid—he had carried around a bit of a death wish since Maureen left him—but he was troubled by the visit.

Not for the first time, Bill Hanrahan realized that Laio Woo was probably dead right, that the old man had said no more than Hanrahan had thought himself.

He rinsed the cups and saucers, put them in the dishwasher, and hurried for the door. He was more than a little late.

By the time Hanrahan got to the Clark Street Station, the lineup was almost over. The small room with the one-way mirror was crowded. Lieberman, Captain Kearney, Harvey Rozier, Kenneth Franklin, and a young female lawyer from the state attorney's office. Hanrahan couldn't remember her name.

No one looked at Hanrahan. Their eyes were fixed beyond the mirror on the small platform where four men stood. Two of the men were cops. One man was a local derelict named Mize. The detectives gave Mize three bucks for every lineup he stood. The last man, second from the left, was the real suspect, George Patniks. Hanrahan had never seen Patniks before, but he knew a frightened man when he saw one.

Bill Hanrahan leaned against the back wall and folded his arms. Lieberman sat next to Rozier and said nothing. In the room beyond, the eyes of George Patniks were fixed on the plate of glass through which he could not see. He was breathing deeply and trying not to show his anxiety, but he was doing one hell of a lousy job.

"Seen enough?" Lieberman asked softly.

"Yes," said Rozier.

"Don't want any of them to step out, turn around, speak again?"

"Not necessary," said Rozier.

Lieberman nodded and knocked twice on the window. Nestor Briggs ushered the four men in the lineup out to the right. Hanrahan switched on the light.

Kenneth Franklin turned to face him with a look of open contempt.

"I would ask that this officer not be present," Franklin said. "My client has already issued an official complaint of harassment against him."

Rozier turned to meet Hanrahan's eyes.

"Sorry, Mr. Franklin, Detective Hanrahan is an investigating officer on this case," said Captain Alan Kearney. "I will be talking to him later in the day concerning your complaint."

Kearney, at forty-one, was the youngest captain in the Chicago Police Department. Until a year ago he had a promising career and the near certainty of becoming the youngest police chief in Chicago history. But a bombshell had hit—a cop had gone mad, barricaded himself in a highrise room, raised hell, and accused Kearney of seducing his wife. The cop on the roof had died and Alan Kearney's ambition had died with him.

Kearney was dark and ruggedly good looking, but fading, a dangerous man who no longer had anything to lose by being honest.

"I think I'll have to insist, Captain," Franklin said.

"And I think I'll have to ask you to back off," said Kearney. "The point of all this is to find the person or persons who murdered Mrs. Rozier, not to get sidetracked by fragile personalities."

"Ken," said Rozier, touching Franklin's arm. "He's right."

Kearney nodded at Lieberman, who said, "Did you recognize any of those men, Mr. Rozier?"

"No," said Rozier with a shake of his head.

"You're sure none of them was the man who came to your door looking for handyman work?" Lieberman went on.

"Positive," said Rozier.

"Harvey, as I believe I told you, has a phenomenal memory for faces," said Franklin.

"Well, then," said Kearney, getting out of his chair, "we'll just have to keep trying."

"We would appreciate that," said Franklin.

"Bill, Abe, in my office. Thank you for coming, gentlemen. We'll keep you informed."

"Thank you," said Rozier.

Kearney left the observation room.

"You know the way out?" asked Lieberman.

"We'll find our way," said Franklin.

"Sergeant," Rozier interrupted, "thanks for trying. If you need me again, I'll be available. Any time, day or night. You're both doing your jobs. Please appreciate that I'm not myself."

"Understood," said Lieberman. "Thanks for coming."

In the hall, walking toward Kearney's office, Lieberman said, "What're you, catching my insomnia? Father Murphy, you look like a wet dog biscuit."

"Lot on my mind, Rabbi," Hanrahan said. "Got a lot on my mind."

"What happened to Chuculo Fernandez?" asked Lieberman.

"Victim's not so sure anymore," said Cadwell without looking up. "Captain says we come up with something sure or we tell the public defender why we're not releasing him. Next time we get Fernandez in here it'll be for murder one. Remember I said it here and I said it first."

Hanrahan met his partner's eyes as they approached Kearney's office.

"Don't look at me like that, Rabbi. I'm sane, sober, and wide awake."

Kearney's office was in the corner of the squad room. It was small, but it was almost soundproof. The captain was seated behind his desk, waiting for them. The detectives sat.

"Well?" asked Kearney.

"I'd say Rozier recognized him."

"So would I," said Kearney.

"So, most likely case," said Lieberman, "is Rozier hired Patniks to kill his wife."

"Doesn't figure," said Kearney.

"Nope," agreed Lieberman. "It doesn't figure. Patniks's not a gun for hire. Certainly not a knife. But who knows?"

"Who knows?" agreed Kearney, looking down at notes on his desk. "Mrs. Rozier was insured for twenty-five thousand. Harvey Rozier spends that in two months on public relations and lunch. The funeral will cost at least five or ten thousand. Mrs. Rozier left everything to him, but that's just about nothing but her half of the house. Doesn't look like a money motive."

"Doesn't look," Lieberman agreed. "Did he fool around?"

"Looking at him, I'd say yes," said Kearney, "but that's not money in the bank. You thinking she was threatening divorce, going for everything he owns?"

"It's happened," said Lieberman.

"Our Harvey, the grieving widower, does not have a hell of a lot she could have taken from him," said Kearney. "He's in a break-even business, scrambling every month to keep it going. Overhead—entertaining, rent, support staff. Our Harvey didn't have much, but he could use some big money."

Kearney bit his lower lip and scanned the notes again.

"Rozier's in good health. No shady deals we can find. Can't say the same for our lawyer, Kenneth Franklin. Franklin is very rich and very sick. Cancer."

"Accounts for some of his attitude," said Lieberman.

"Might," said Kearney, looking up at Hanrahan. "What the hell were you trying to do last night?"

"We," said Lieberman. "Bill and I agreed he'd go talk to Rozier."

"At ten at night? The time alone, without an emergency, is enough to give some weight to Franklin and Rozier's screams about harassment."

"He's guilty of something, and—" said Hanrahan.

"And you're sorry you did it," Kearney finished.

"Absolutely," said Hanrahan.

"The bottle of ipecac," Kearney said, dismissing the reprimand. "No fingerprints on it. Not a trace. Not a smudge. Wiped clean. Know anyone who wipes medicine bottles before they put them away?"

"An odd fetish," said Lieberman.

"Evidence says the other bottles in Dana Rozier's closet were handled by her. Best possibility here?"

"Rozier wiped his prints off the bottle and put it in his wife's drawer," said Hanrahan.

"Rozier or the killer. Can you think of any reason a break-in burglar who just committed a murder would wipe fingerprints off a bottle of ipecac?" Kearney paused. "Neither can I. So why didn't Rozier throw the bottle away?"

"Smart enough to know that we might find traces in her," said Hanrahan. "We find it. Looks like she kept it hidden. It's all a puzzle to the grieving spouse."

"So," said Kearney, "what have we got?"

"*Bubkes,*" said Lieberman.

"Right. We've got nothing," said Kearney. "A bottle of throw-up medicine with no fingerprints, a suspect who we think recognizes a burglar in a lineup but says he doesn't, a suspect with no apparent motive and an alibi. What do we do?"

"We find some evidence," said Lieberman.

Iago Simms was grinning, but unless you knew him as well as Dalbert and Lonny did, there was no way of knowing. Iago's face sagged to the left and his teeth were exposed on the right.

"Yes," said Iago, holding up the pistol he had found in the glove compartment of the car they had just borrowed from Reno the drug dealer.

Getting into the garage had been harder than they thought it would be. Three locks on the door. It wasn't daylight yet so they were reasonably sure no one had seen them. Lonny was all for giving up on the whole crazy idea, but there was no way he'd let Dalbert and Iago know it.

"Fuck, kick it down," Lonny had said, and Dalbert hadn't hesitated. Over two hundred pounds hit the garage door. It gave but didn't break. Dalbert turned to Lonny.

"Again," Lonny said, looking around to see if any lights were going on in the houses behind them.

"Put some shit in it this time," Iago encouraged.

And Dalbert tried again, throwing himself against the door. It cracked and spat open, cracking against the wooden wall and almost hitting Dalbert in the face when it bounced back.

"Get the garage door up fast," Lonny said.

Iago moved to the maroon Chrysler and opened the driver's side door, heading straight for the wiring under the dash. Dalbert hit the switch, opening the garage doors. They slid open smoothly in spite of the breaks.

"Hurry up," Lonny cried.

"Got it. Got it. Got it," called Iago. The engine purred awake. "There."

The three of them scrambled into the car, Lonny driving, and sped down the alley.

"Hey, we didn't close the door," Dalbert cried, looking through the rear window.

"Don't matter," said Lonny.

"Why?"

" 'Cause," said Iago, turning in the front seat, "you kicked the door to shit. No way we can get it back and not have some nigger fool with a sawed-off waiting for us. We do the job and drop the car wherever. That right, Lonny?"

"That's right," Lonny said.

Iago had turned on the radio. Some woman was singing about men being no good. Lonny reached over and turned the radio off. It was then that Iago opened the glove compartment and found the gun.

"Our lucky day, damn sure," said Iago, aiming the gun out the window with one eye closed.

It didn't feel lucky to Lonny. The day already felt like bad news, but there was no going back. He drove without talking, drove within the speed limit north on Lake Shore Drive, past Lincoln Park and Lake Michigan following them on the right, luxury high-rises beyond the park to the left.

Lonny had trouble finding the windshield wiper switch and almost lost control of the car, but after three false tries, he hit a button and the wipers came on, spreading the thin layer of rain into the morning.

Twenty-two minutes from the time they left the garage, Lonny was parking on Argyle across from Jacob Berry's office.

"He there yet?" asked Dalbert.

"Don't look it," said Iago.

"What we do?" asked Dalbert.

"Wait, that's what we do," said Lonny. "We just wait. When he comes, someone should stay in the car, be ready. We got no time to fool around disconnecting and shit like that, you got that?"

"No lie," said Iago. "But I'm not stayin' in the car. Dalbert can stay."

"No way," said Dalbert angrily.

If he could have trusted the two of them, Lonny would have sighed his put-upon sigh, his I-don't-know-how-I-put-up-with-you sigh. Then he would have stayed in the car. It had felt bad when they got to the garage and it didn't feel any better now, sitting there waiting for the doctor to come to work. Shit, they'd all go in.

"Maybe we can just like break in up there and look for

the drugs, money, all that shit. See what I'm sayin'?" Dalbert tried.

"We wait for him," Lonny said, imitating that bald dude Hawk used to be on "Spencer" on TV. "We wait."

Jacob Berry woke up that morning not sure whether he felt worse or better about coming to Chicago. The sky was dark and drizzly, no better or worse than East Lansing but maybe a little grittier.

He showered, shaved, dressed, had a large glass of orange juice—not from concentrate—a cup of decaf Folger's, and a toasted poppy seed bagel as he listened to the radio.

Rain, rain, more rain, and then rain again. Killers of little girls in the news. Fathers going mad and taking their children hostage. Bus crashes. No leads yet in the knifing of the woman in a good neighborhood, in her own home. And this was just in the city. Dr. Berry changed the station. Rock music. He changed it again. Oldies. Chubby Checker.

Bagels were better in Chicago. Food was better. People were not.

He rinsed the dishes and put them neatly into the dishwasher before he walked to the front door, picked up his briefcase, opened it on the table, and checked to be sure the gun was there, reassuring, ready. He considered putting the weapon in his pocket, but that was too awkward and heavy. When he got to the office he would remove the gun and put it in the drawer.

Jacob was ready to meet the day. He encountered no one on the elevator, which was fine with him. He didn't want to tell people he was a doctor and have them give him a strange, questioning look that said, "If you're a doctor, what're you living in this building for? I've got no choice, but a doctor?"

Jacob didn't know the names of anyone in the building, though he did recognize a few faces.

He made it through the small, dank-smelling lobby and onto the street, where he found his '90 Toyota unscratched and not broken into. It wasn't much of a car, but he didn't want to go through the anguish of dealing with the insurance company.

Jacob was only ten minutes from his office. He had a paid parking space behind the Golden Wing Vietnamese Restaurant. For thirty dollars a month, the Hee family would keep an eye on the vehicle for him and provide him a reasonably certain parking space in a heavily trafficked neighborhood. In East Lansing he had a free space with his name on it right outside the clinic.

Mrs. Hee came out when he had parked and waved at him as she dropped a plastic bag of garbage into one of the containers chained to the wall. Jacob waved back.

A distant el train rumbled as he came through the alley and headed toward his office. Cars already lined the street, some of them belonging to people who lived nearby, others belonging to early customers or the people who worked in and owned the shops. A shiny maroon Pontiac Grand Prix idled across the street. There seemed to be no one in the car.

Jacob unlocked the downstairs door, flipped on the hall lights, went up the stairs, and opened his office. When he hit the switch he knew that all was well. Everything was where it should be.

He moved into the office examining room, opened his briefcase, and put his gun in his desk, leaving the drawer just slightly open.

He checked his watch. Nine. He had an appointment at nine and another at ten, both police physicals. Jacob went to the window and pulled up the shade, just a little, enough to let in a dusty stream of gray light but not enough to allow anyone to look in from the el platform or a passing train.

His nine o'clock was late. He heard someone try the front door. As usual, Jacob had locked it. Someone knocked.

"Coming," he called, adjusting his starched lab coat.

Jacob was sure it was his nine o'clock physical. He never considered any other possibility as he opened the door and saw the three young men in front of him. They had come. The ones who had looked through the window. Jacob Berry's knees started to buckle.

One of the three, a little one with a twisted face, held a gun to Jacob's belly. A second one, short and solid, held a knife in his hand. The third, tall with a dark, angry scar through his eyebrow said, "Back in."

The little one pushed Jacob back with the barrel of his gun and the one with the scar closed the door behind him.

"Now," said the big one with the scar. "You go fill a bag with money, drugs, everything you got, and fast, or we operate on you, and believe me, motherfucker, we don't know shit about surgery."

Jacob couldn't speak. His legs carried him backward but threatened to buckle.

"I've only got a few drugs and the money in my wallet, about forty dollars," he said, reaching for his wallet.

The heavy-set one with the knife wrenched the wallet from his hand and shoved it in his pocket.

"You lyin'," the tall one said. "Find somethin', and fast. We got no time to spend here."

"But I don't . . ."

"Find it or you're dog food," said the little one with the gun.

"OK, all right," Jacob said, backing up. "I've got something."

The one with the knife grinned and Jacob eased around the desk to the partly open drawer.

"Move your ass," cried the one with the gun.

And then all hell broke loose. The nine o'clock appointment, a patrolman named Matthews, who also happened to be black, came through the unlocked outer door, noticed by no one in the office and noticing nothing unusual. Matthews had a fear of needles. He just wanted to get the physical over with.

When he stepped into the door of the inner office, he saw the three young men, saw the gun and knife, and met the frightened eyes of Dr. Berry behind the desk.

Matthews went for his gun. Iago Simms turned and fired. Jacob Berry groped for the weapon in his desk, pulled it out, aimed in the general direction of the three hold-up men, and began pulling the trigger.

Someone screamed.

Panic in the Streets

Lieberman and Hanrahan had just moved to their desks, which faced each other next to the heating duct. Today was just cold enough for the automatic thermostat to kick on the heat. Hot air baked the right side of Lieberman's face. His phone was ringing.

"Lieberman," he said, answering the call.

"Nervous guy on the phone says he's got to talk to you," said Nestor Briggs. "Says he's a rabbi. Says it's important."

"Put him through," Lieberman said, looking across at his partner with a shake of his head.

"Lieberman," Abe said again.

"Lieberman?" asked Rabbi Nathanson.

"Yes, what can I do for you, Rabbi? I haven't had a chance to call my lawyer or discuss this further with my wife, but—"

"I've made a list," Nathanson said, and Lieberman imagined the *langa-loksch*, the long noodle of a man, with an unfurling parchment scroll before him.

"A list?"

"Problems which must be remedied, alterations which must be made before we can move into the house."

"Alterations?"

"And some necessary remodeling," confirmed Rabbi Nathanson. "All wallpaper removed and replaced with paint conforming to my specifications. Carpets out and wooden floors sanded and treated. Complete reslating of the roof and new electrical outlets throughout."

"You want me to pay for this?" asked Lieberman.

"It is your responsibility," said Rabbi Nathanson.

"I thought you loved the house just the way it is."

"I do, but it requires some maintenance to make it livable," said the rabbi.

"I don't think we can do business, Rabbi," Lieberman said.

"We have a good faith contract," Nathanson said sternly. "I gave you a check. There were witnesses."

"Your check is going back to you in the mail tonight. No, better yet, my wife is dropping it off at B'nai Shalom this afternoon."

"That is not acceptable, Lieberman. This is a breach of contract—no, it is a breach of faith," said Nathanson.

"Breaking a commandment is a breach of faith," said Lieberman calmly. "Giving your check back is common sense."

"I have a lawyer," said Nathanson. "Two lawyers, Greenblatt and Greenblatt."

"Send in the Greenblatts," said Lieberman. "Now, I've got to go find a murderer. Someone cut up a woman. That's a little more important right now."

"Dana Rozier," said Nathanson. "I saw on the news. Are the Roziers Jewish?"

"I don't think so, Rabbi," said Lieberman.

"Thank God," said Nathanson.

"My wife's returning the check. Your lawyer and my lawyer can get together and bill us so we can both be sure of losing money on this deal. Good-bye, Rabbi."

"It would be easier to be reasonable," Rabbi Nathanson tried with great self-assurance.

"We agree on that," said Lieberman and hung up the phone.

"What was that?" asked Hanrahan.

Lieberman tapped his finger on the phone and changed the subject.

"Let's switch. I play nice guy with Rozier. You play bad guy with Patniks."

"You think we could be wrong on this one, Rabbi?" asked Hanrahan.

"On Rozier? No, Father Murphy, he's at the top of the

136

short list. Patniks, I'd say he didn't kill her, but he knows something. Maybe Rozier paid him and he backed out at the last second. And our Harvey has a hell of an alibi. Clean."

"Then who killed Dana Rozier?" Hanrahan asked.

Lieberman shrugged. His phone was ringing again. He picked it up and heard Bess say, "Abraham, Rabbi Nathanson just called me demanding about ten thousand dollars in changes to the house."

"You know where the check is?"

"In my hand. I'd like to tear it into little pieces."

"Put it in an envelope and drop it off at B'nai Shalom."

"I'm Federal Expressing it with a return receipt requested," Bess said.

"Better yet," said Lieberman. "I gotta go."

"Lisa wants to talk to you."

"Bess . . ."

"Dad." Lisa's voice, as calm and resolute as that of the mad rabbi.

"Lisa," he said, looking at Hanrahan, who got up and moved toward the coffee across the room.

"We've got to talk, today."

"I'll try to get home early," he said.

"Today, not tonight."

"I'll be at the T and L for lunch, maybe two, maybe a little earlier."

"I'll be there."

"You're not working?"

"Not today," she said.

Lisa hung up the phone as Hanrahan returned with two cups of coffee. He handed one to Lieberman and sat down.

"With caffeine?" Lieberman asked, looking at the cup, which had AMSTERDAM CRUISES printed on it in purple letters.

Hanrahan shrugged. Lieberman drank.

"Let's go see if we can make a hole or two in our grief-stricken husband's story."

"If . . ." Hanrahan began shifting in his chair to get a few more inches away from the inferno belching out of the heating vent.

"Hold it," Lieberman said, picking up on something Francis Acardo was saying on the phone a desk away.

"Francis," Lieberman called.

Acardo put his hand over the receiver and said, "Shooting, at Doc Berry's office. Officer down. Cars are rolling. As usual, confusion reigns."

Both Hanrahan and Lieberman got up and, without speaking, ran for the squad room door. They were less than twelve minutes from Argyle Street in normal traffic. They made it with flashing lights in eight. Black and whites, three of them, with lights flashing, were blocking the street. People, most of them Oriental, lined the sidewalk, held back by two female uniformed officers. Lieberman pulled around the police car blocking Broadway and double-parked.

The rain had stopped, at least for now. The street was wet and the clouds gray and grumbling.

They moved past the officers holding the crowd back and saw a young patrolman kneeling over the contorted body of a young black boy. The dead boy's hands were clutching his stomach as if he had a terrible cramp and his face was distorted in agony. He had curled up like a fetus to die.

"This one's dead, Abe," the kneeling patrolman said. "A knife in his pocket, two bucks and some change. No wallet, no ID."

"Officer down?" asked Hanrahan.

The kneeling patrolman pointed to the entrance of Jacob Berry's office.

A clot of people, all police, seemed to be sitting down for a coffee break on the steps. An ambulance wailed outside and not far away. And somewhere up the stairway a man was screaming in anger.

A third female officer, Shea, stood up when she saw the detectives, and Lieberman could now see that an older cop at the bottom of the stairs, Hugh Jensen, was cradling the head of Guy Matthews in his lap. Matthews was covered in blood. Matthews was gasping for air, his chest heaving.

"Lung, I think," said Jensen. "Looks worse than it is. Maybe. If that goddamn ambulance would just get here and clear the blood . . ."

"What happened?" Hanrahan asked.

The voice above, words unclear, was screaming again.

"Looks like a shoot-out in the doc's office upstairs," said Shea. "Perp down up there. Two of them ran out in the street. Matthews followed them. He was already shot."

She pointed to a trail of blood on the stairs.

"Seems they had a car waiting," said Jensen, "but someone stole it while they were in the doc's office. The dead one out there had a gun. Matthews shot him. The other one ran. I don't like the way he's breathing," he said, looking down at the wounded officer.

Matthews was gasping for air now, eyes closed. Hanrahan stepped forward, knelt, and pried the wounded officer's mouth open with his fingers. He turned Matthews' head down to the right and reached into his mouth to pull out a squirming clot of blood. Then he put his mouth to that of the gasping man and began to suck out blood, spitting it onto Jensen's shoes. Officer Shea bit her lower lip but didn't turn away.

The ambulance was close now, wailing just outside the door. Lieberman went up the stairs. The screamer was at it again. Inside Dr. Berry's office/examining room Abe Lieberman saw a solid tree stump of a young black man, his hands cuffed behind his back, being restrained by two uniformed officers. The young man was seated in the same chair Lieberman had sat in two days ago but kept trying to stand. Blood was oozing through a hole in his right pants leg.

"That fool," the young man screamed in a high voice, looking across the room at Jacob Berry, who sat, stunned, behind his desk. On top of the briefcase before him sat the gun that Jacob had purchased the day before. "Where's Lonny? What you doin' with Iago? Man, I want me a lawyer. I want me a doctor, but not that fool."

"Shut up," said one of the two cops through clenched teeth, pushing the screaming man back down on the chair. The cop was big. Both cops were big. They had to be to keep the screaming man down.

Lieberman moved to Jacob Berry, who was staring at the screaming young man as if he heard nothing, as if he had just been awakened and was trying to make some sense of the chaos that greeted him.

"You all right, Doc?" Lieberman said, touching his shoulder.

Jacob nodded. "I shot him," he said, removing his glasses and looking up at Lieberman.

"Yeah," said Lieberman.

"No, not him," Jacob said, looking at the angry young man across the room. "The policeman shot him. I . . . I think . . . I know I shot the policeman. I should help him. I'm a doctor. I should do something."

"You wouldn't be much good," said Lieberman. "Where'd you get the gun?"

"Gun? Bought it from somebody, a man, yesterday. I was afraid."

Lieberman sighed. The young black man had gone sullenly silent after uttering one more, "Damn fool."

"So you bought an illegal weapon," said Lieberman. "I told you I'd help you."

"Couldn't wait," said Berry, throwing up his hands.

A scrambling out the door and down the stairs, voices of paramedics.

"I've got to help," Jacob Berry said, wiping his eyes with his sleeve and rising.

"Sure," said Lieberman, stepping out of the way.

Jacob Berry didn't glance at the restrained man who had cursed him. Instead Dr. Berry rushed to help the man who may have saved his life, the man he had shot. Lieberman rubbed a finger across his mustache and stepped over to the seated young man.

"You get me a fuckin' doctor," the young man screamed. "I'm bleedin'."

"His name is Albert Davis," said one of the officers.

"Social Security card, four dollars, a condom, and a photo ID from a drug store in his wallet. Address is on MLK Drive near Michael Reese Hospital."

Lieberman nodded and turned to Albert Davis.

"One of your friends is dead," he said.

"Dead?" Dalbert said, looking at each of the two uniformed policemen for confirmation. "Which one?"

"What do this Iago and Lonny look like?" Lieberman said.

"How you know their names?" Dalbert said in panic.

"You told them to us a minute ago, Albert," Lieberman said calmly. "You want to know which one is dead and which one got away?"

"Got away? Iago's a skinny kid. Lonny's big, got a scar like lightning over his eye."

"Last names, Albert," Lieberman pressed.

"Nobody calls me Albert. Dalbert. I'm Dalbert. Get me a damn doctor. Who's dead?"

"Names, Dalbert?"

"I don't know no last names," the young man said sullenly as a paramedic in blue hurried into the room.

"Iago's dead," Lieberman said.

Dalbert bit his lower lip, nodded, and went silent as the paramedic knelt to rip away his trousers and examine the bullet wound.

"Touch nothing and call Evidence," Lieberman told the two officers. "Leave the weapon where it is."

Both cops nodded.

There was nothing on the steps as Lieberman walked down, nothing but a trail of Guy Matthews's blood. Outside, the door to the ambulance was just closing. A second ambulance was rolling down the street.

The crowd had grown. Jensen and Shea had moved forward to help control it, but the sight of Bill Hanrahan, blood covering his mouth and face, was enough to restrain even the most adventurous of the gawkers. Hanrahan was doing his best to remove the blood with a handkerchief, but he wasn't making much headway.

"How you doin', Father Murphy?"

Hanrahan nodded.

"I'll be fine, Rabbi."

"Dead kid's name is Iago," said Lieberman, looking at the sheet that now covered the body. "One that got away is Lonny. I've got a description."

Jensen walked back to the detectives and said, "Woman in the crowd, owns the restaurant over there. She says the one that got away ran through the alley going south. She thinks he had a gun in his hand."

"Thanks," said Lieberman.

Jensen glanced at Hanrahan's ghoulish face and moved back to help control the crowd.

Police cars were pouring in now, lights flashing. The sound of the siren diminished as the ambulance carrying the fallen officer sped toward Edgewater Hospital. Applegate and Acardo piled out of one of the cars.

"Where's Berry?" asked Lieberman.

"Went in the ambulance with Matthews," said Hanrahan.

"Let's go in the restaurant and get you washed up," said Lieberman.

"He's not that far ahead of us, Abe," Hanrahan said, moving toward the restaurant.

"I'll make the calls," said Lieberman as the crowd parted to let the hulking, bloody policeman through.

Lieberman brought Applegate and Acardo up to date and left them to pick up the pieces and put the story together.

Lieberman went to his car and made the calls. Comb the neighborhood looking for a young black man with a lightning scar through his eyebrow. Probably armed. Definitely dangerous. Try to head off the north- and southbound el trains and search them. Check the buses. Check the cabs. It wouldn't be fast enough, Lieberman knew, but it had to be done. The young man named Lonny was probably out of the neighborhood by now. Alone, afraid, and armed. A very bad combination.

Lieberman got an idea. He called the Chapultapec Restaurant on North Avenue.

"*Sí,*" a man's voice answered.

"*Es* Emiliano *allá?*" asked Lieberman.

"¿Quién es esto?"

"Lieberman. *Es necesario que hablo con* Emiliano *inmediatamente."*

"Emiliano no está aquí."

"Búscale. Tiene prisa. Diga que tengo algo a decir de Chuculo Fernandez. *¿Comprende?"*

"Comprendo. Su número?"

Lieberman gave the number of the T & L Deli and told the man on the phone that he'd be there in fifteen minutes.

"Bueno," said the man and hung up.

The car door opened and Hanrahan, his hair and jacket front wet, slid inside.

"You clean up good, Murph."

"Compulsive cleaner, Rabbi."

"I know. You up for an early lunch?"

Lieberman put the car in gear as Hanrahan smiled and nodded.

Fifteen minutes later they parked on Devon, half a block from Maish's T & L. The clouds complained but didn't burst as they moved past Kim the Korean's Devon Television/VCR Repair Shop, the Dollar Store, also owned by Kim, and the Pistoki brothers' fruit market.

The T & L was empty except for Maish behind the counter reading a book and one Alter Cocker, the red-headed Al Bloombach, who sat alone at the table reserved for the old men, a coffee and half-eaten bagel in front of him. Something was cooking for the lunch crowd. A cabbage pot. Lieberman was sure it was a forbidden cabbage pot. Torture inflicted by Dr. Jacob Berry, who, when he came out of his minishock, would face a far greater torture.

"Where's everybody?" Lieberman asked.

"Baseball game. Syd's son rented a van. They all go to the ball game," explained Al Bloombach.

"And you?" asked Lieberman, moving with Hanrahan to the counter and sitting on the red leatherette stool.

"My sciatic," said Al. "Who wants to sit in the rain with sciatic? And to tell the truth, I'm not such a big baseball fan. Give me the football and I'll watch till the last fumble."

Maish looked up from his book and met his brother's eyes.

"How's Yetta?" asked Abe.

"She's Yetta," said Maish with a shrug.

"How's Maish?"

"You know. Nothing Bothers Maish," Maish said. "What can I get you, William?"

"Coffee. What's good on rye today?"

"A Sandy Koufax. Pastrami, chopped liver, and cole slaw with a pickle," said Maish.

"Heartburn heaven," Al Bloombach called.

"I'll take it," said Hanrahan.

"Abe?" asked Maish.

"Seltzer and toast me a bagel. No butter."

"Diet again?" asked Maish.

"Cholesterol's a little high," said Abe.

Maish called the order back to Manuel in the kitchen and turned his homely bulldog face to his brother.

"We're coming over Friday for dinner," Maish said. "Bess invited."

"Dinner and services," said Abe.

"I'm not going to services anymore," said Maish, finding a spot on the counter that may have been a smudge of mustard. He attacked it with a wet cloth. "I'm not on speaking terms with God right now. When your only son is gunned down by a crazy man in the street for no reason, you tend to get that way. It's reasonable. What d'you think, William?"

Maish poured a cup of coffee and set it down in front of Hanrahan.

"I'm a Catholic," he said.

Maish nodded as if that made perfect sense.

"A Catholic. You're not supposed to get mad at God. You are supposed to make love, not war. Well, I heard on the radio something that made sense, from an Arab no less. The opposite of war is not love. The opposite of war is peace. You don't have to love your enemy. It's not reasonable. Peace, now that's another story. God wants to make peace with me he knows where to find me, but so far he hasn't come knocking and he hasn't sent me a telegram."

"Maish," Abe tried.

"Seltzer and a bagel and a Sandy Koufax. I know."

The phone rang as Maish shuffled away in search of seltzer. Lieberman leaned over the counter, groped for the phone, found it on the fourth ring, and placed it in front of him on the counter.

"Hello," he said. "Maish's T and L."

"Viejo," came the voice of Emiliano "El Perro" Del Sol, the leader of the Tentáculos, the gang that ruled North Avenue when there were enough of them out of jail.

"Emiliano, I've got a deal for you."

Lieberman imagined the slightly mad El Perro sitting in the Chapultapec in near darkness or in his recently acquired bingo parlor on Crawford Avenue.

"I got a deal for you?" said El Perro. "Ain't you gonna ask how I'm doin'? How's my mother? How's my sister? How's Piedras?"

"How are they?" Lieberman asked as Maish placed a large glass of seltzer before him.

"Bueno," said El Perro. "My family. I take care of my family. You know that. I take care of you. You're like an uncle to me, a crazy uncle, *Tío Loco*."

Lieberman had developed a reputation for recklessness on the streets when he worked out of the North Avenue before being transferred to Clark Street.

Part of the reputation was earned. Most of it was calculated. But Emiliano Del Sol had believed all of it as a kid and respected the old Jew policeman who was every bit as wild as El Perro himself.

"Chuculo Fernandez," said Lieberman after taking a sip of seltzer. "He's like a brother too?"

"More like a cousin, you know?"

"He's in trouble, Emiliano."

"*Yo sé,* Viejo. *¿Qué tiene a decir?*"

"*Quiero a ayudarle,*" said Lieberman. "I'm looking for a young black man named Lonny. Doesn't have a last name. I'm working on that. He's got a scar running through

145

his right eyebrow. Runs with a pair named Iago and Dalbert. Iago's dead. Dalbert's bleeding and Lonny's on the streets with a gun. Dalbert's a South Sider. Lonny figures to be the same."

"We find him and . . . ?"

"Chuculo walks," said Lieberman, looking at Hanrahan, who was accepting a plate with a fat, heavenly smelling sandwich.

"*Vero?* He just walks. You got that kinda *cojones*, Viejo? Let my man Chuculo walk?"

"You got my word, Emiliano. But it's got to be fast and I don't want Lonny hurt. You turn him up by tomorrow morning and you can come pick up Chuculo Fernandez and have him in front of the Chapultepec with his knife in his pocket by three. We find him first and there's no deal."

"I like you, Viejo," said El Perro.

"It is the knowledge of that affection that sustains me in trying moments," said Lieberman.

El Perro laughed. "You are some crazy son of a bitch," he said.

"I try to keep the troops amused," said Lieberman. "Tomorrow morning."

"He's alive, we find him. I'll put *Los Negros* on this."

Los Negros were the Oliveros, two black brothers and a cousin, from Panama City. *Los Negros* could go on the South Side looking for Lonny. The rest of the Tentáculos would get cold looks, no answers, and a ten-to-one certainty that someone would get hurt.

"Sounds good to me," said Lieberman.

El Perro hung up the phone and Maish brought the toasted bagel. Hanrahan laughed and said, "You're a devious one, Rabbi."

"What?" asked Maish.

"We have to let Fernandez go by tomorrow no matter what," Lieberman explained, looking longingly at the sandwich his partner was downing. "Our witness backed out."

"How about an omelette with Egg Beaters, onions, some mushrooms?" Maish asked.

Lieberman shrugged in resignation.

Maish nodded and called back the order.

"How are you doing, Father Murph?"

"I'm pleased to announce that I've regained my appetite."

"I didn't know you'd lost it."

"Briefly," said Hanrahan, taking a bite of his pickle. "The truth, Abraham. You think Iris and I could make it? I mean, married?"

"Who knows?" said Lieberman, finishing the last of his bagel.

"Marriage is an institution," called Al Bloombach. "A mental institution."

Al chuckled, proud of himself and sorry he had no Alter Cockers around to appreciate his joke.

"You're a big help, Rabbi," said Hanrahan.

"Marry her," said Lieberman, holding up his empty glass for a refill.

"I'm an irresponsible Irish cop with a drinking problem that might come back when I'm not on guard. She's Chinese and she'll be shunned by her people."

"Don't marry her," said Lieberman.

"That's your advice? Marry her or don't marry her?"

"That's my advice too," said Maish, shuffling to the kitchen.

"If you have kids . . ." Bloombach called.

"No kids," said Hanrahan. "We're both too old for kids."

"Father Murph," Lieberman said. "If I don't give advice, I can't be blamed for giving bad advice if it goes wrong. I won't get credit for good advice either, but that's easier to live with."

Hanrahan nodded.

Maish schlepped the omelette from the kitchen and placed it in front of Lieberman. It didn't smell half bad.

"After we eat—" Lieberman began.

"Patniks for me. Rozier for you," said Hanrahan.

"And tea for two," called Al Bloombach.

"That man is desperately in need of companionship," said Lieberman, probing his omelette with a fork.

Behind the two policemen the T & L door swung open and someone said, "Hello, Uncle Maish."

Lisa. Lieberman had forgotten about his daughter.

"I'm on my way, Rabbi," said Hanrahan, counting off five dollars and dropping them on the counter as he stood.

"Lisa, I'm going through the motions," said Maish.

"How are you, Lisa?" Bill Hanrahan said, abandoning his partner to his family.

"All right," she said, moving past him and sitting next to her father.

"Good to hear it," Hanrahan said. "See you at the station, Abe."

"At the station," Lieberman echoed.

"What can I get you, Lisa?" Maish asked. "Manny's almost got the pickled whitefish ready."

"Coffee, toast," she said, looking at her father.

Lieberman turned and met his daughter's eyes. She looked serious.

"Abe," she said. "Todd's going to marry her. He wants the divorce and he's going to marry her."

"I know," said Lieberman, realizing even as he spoke that he had made a massive error.

"You knew and you didn't tell me?"

"He mentioned it when he brought the kids home last night," said Abe, giving up his search for anything meaningful in the omelette. "I haven't had a chance to see you."

"I can't stay in the same city with them," she said.

"It's a big city with lots of suburbs," Abe said. "You give them north of Howard Street and you take the rest."

"That's not funny," she said, watching her uncle place a hot coffee mug in front of her. "How's Aunt Yetta?"

"She's Aunt Yetta," said Maish, moving away with a shrug.

"You should help him, Abe," Lisa whispered, picking up her coffee cup.

"I'm trying, Lisa," he said. "What's the issue?"

"Issue?"

"You, your mother. On the phone. I know an issue when I hear one coming."

"I can't stay in Chicago," she said. "There's too much . . . I can't stay."

Lieberman wished he could dangle the prospect of Dr. Jacob Berry before his daughter, but Berry's eligibility had been seriously compromised. In fact, the odds were good that Dr. Berry's medical license was in jeopardy and that, if Matthews died, involuntary manslaughter and possession of an illegal weapon were in his future. Lieberman's mind raced for a possible substitute. He even considered Alan Kearney, then immediately rejected the idea.

"Where are you going?"

"San Francisco," she said. "I've always wanted to live in San Francisco, you know that."

Abe knew nothing of the kind, but he nodded in agreement.

"When?" he asked.

"Soon, next month. Right after Barry's bar mitzvah. I want you to tell Todd that I agree to the divorce. I want nothing from him, not even support for the children."

"I'll tell him."

"And you can send me whatever papers need to be signed."

"I will," he promised. "Anything else?"

"Yes, I talked to Mom about this. She said it was all right with her if it's all right with you."

Lieberman could feel it coming. He faced his daughter in the hope of intimidating her into backing down, but the past thirty-five years told him it was hopeless.

"You want to leave the kids with us," he said.

"For awhile," she said. "I think I can get a job with a pharmaceutical company in Oakland, but the cost of living there, transportation, setting things up . . ."

"Todd would help," Abe said.

Lisa looked deeply into her steaming coffee and shook her head.

"I don't want anything from Todd."

No, you want something from me and your mother, Abe thought, but was wise enough this time to say nothing. And besides, the prospect of having Barry and Melisa around without Lisa to tell him the proper way to treat them was tempting.

"Let's set a time limit," Lieberman said.

"Just six months," she said. "And I'll come back and visit on holiday weekends. I can get a special rate if I book in advance."

"Six months," Abe repeated.

"Maybe a little less, maybe a little more. I couldn't stand being away from Barry and Melisa for long."

"I'm more than sixty years old, Melisa. Your mother's . . . a little younger."

Her eyes met his, moist, pleading, hopeful, a look he hadn't seen from her in almost thirty years.

"Fine," he said with a sigh.

She hugged him, something she had done only once in the last twenty years, the night after Maish's son David was murdered.

"What?" asked Maish, coming with coffee refills.

"Lisa's moving to San Francisco," Abe said. "Bess and I are keeping the kids till she gets settled."

The door behind Lieberman opened and someone said, "What smells so good, Maish?"

"Boiled cabbage, pickled whitefish," said Maish.

The rush hour lunch had begun.

"Gregor, what are you doin'?"

When he had returned from the lineup, George Patniks had told his mother as little as possible and then gone down to his room to pace and listen to Sally Jessie and his mother laugh above him.

He tried to think about painting, a new painting, something light for a change—trees, a park, kids, oranges, anything—but nothing took shape. He paced.

Rozier had been behind that mirror, looking at him, gauging him, knowing that the police suspected something. Was Rozier home now? Or was he in his car searching for George, a long, sharp knife tucked into his belt?

Then, after a full hour of pacing and well into Oprah, George pulled out the painting of the murderer and the dying woman, packed it in cardboard, and taped it tight, then packed a bag and went upstairs.

"I'm going to Seattle, Ma," he said. "I'll call Tommy, tell him to look out for you. Anyone comes looking for me, you tell 'em I went to Seattle for an art show."

"With one painting you're going to an art show?"

"I shipped the others."

"When? Where you ship the others?"

"Last week. You were sleeping."

"Gregor, what's wrong?"

"The damn television is too loud, that's what's wrong. I can't think. I can't paint. I'll be gone a week, maybe two. Promise. I gotta go. I'll call."

"What's wrong, Gregor?" she repeated, summoning the energy to rise from her chair.

"I'm going, Ma," he said. "I'll call you."

He left her standing heavily in front of the serious face of Oprah, who was talking about children with some rare disease.

"I'll call," he repeated at the door. "Don't worry."

He opened the door, took a step down, and found himself facing one of the cops he had seen after the lineup, a big cop with a pink face.

"Suitcase in one hand, what looks like a wrapped-up painting in the other," said Bill Hanrahan. "Being a good detective, I'm gonna conclude that you're taking a little trip."

"I was going to call my parole officer before I left," George said. "I've got a chance to make a big sale in Seattle."

"My partner thinks the Seattle stuff is a bunch of bullshit, George," Hanrahan said with a smile. "Why don't we go back in and talk about this morning, maybe look at some of your work? Abe says you've got talent."

"I'll miss my bus," George pleaded.

"That you will," agreed Hanrahan sadly, hearing his father's voice. "That you will."

* * *

Eupatniaks, that was the name, Harvey Rozier remembered. He had tried every Patniks in the book—well, the three listed—but now he was searching for a Eupatniaks. He wasn't sure of how to spell it, but how many variations could there be?

In five minutes, Harvey had narrowed the list down to three names. He called the first and asked if George was there.

"George doesn't live here," the woman said. "His brother Tommy lives here. You want George, you call him at Wanda's."

"I don't have the number."

The woman on the other end gave a put-upon sigh and gave Harvey a phone number.

"I'm sorry," he said, turning on the charm, "but do you have the address?"

He waited for her to question his request, but she simply gave him an address on Clyborne.

"Thanks," he said and hung up.

Simple, it had been so simple.

Betty was sitting in the living room waiting for him when he came down. She had a magazine in her hand. She dropped it to the floor and got up.

"I've got to go out, Betty," he said. "For a little while."

"But Harvey . . ." she began.

He smiled and stepped forward to embrace her but stopped when he realized someone else was in the room. He turned to face Lieberman, who sat drinking coffee.

"If you're in a hurry," said the detective, "I'll go with you."

"I'm . . . no. It can wait. Just going into the office to take my mind off of things, take care of a problem the staff is having trouble with."

Lieberman nodded and looked at Betty Franklin, who was definitely on the edge and about to fall after Rozier's indiscreet move.

"Good, then let's talk about the lineup this morning." said Lieberman.

Mean Streets

Lonny Wayne got off the Sheridan bus a stop before Irving Park and headed for Broadway. He wasn't sure where he was going, but he was heading south and the general direction of home.

A cop car had passed the bus just before Irving. Lonny had slid down in his seat, certain that an old black man pretending to read a newspaper was watching him. When the cop car passed, Lonny turned to face the man with the newspaper. The man kept his face in the paper. The bus wasn't crowded: three old women and the man with the paper.

Through the front window of the bus Lonny could see the cop car slowing up. Lonny pulled the cord and the bus eased up at the next corner. Lonny got up languidly, wanting to run, forcing himself to stay cool, standing in front of the fuckin' door the driver was taking forever to open.

Then it opened with a clack and he leaped off. As the bus pulled away, the old man with the newspaper looked down at him through the window with something that looked like pity.

Lonny hurried toward Broadway, the gun in his jacket pocket bumping against his side.

He'd walk back to the neighborhood, sixty blocks. Not get trapped on a bus or an el. Walk back and then ... what?

Iago was dead for sure. Damn. A cop. Walks right in. Gun in his hand, shooting. And that motherfuck doctor. He's shooting. And Iago, he's shooting. And the cop goes down and Dalbert screams. Lonny had leaped over the fallen, groaning cop with Iago behind him. They'd gone down the stairs, tripping over each other. And then in the street, Iago waving the gun. The damn car gone. And then the shot and Iago was down.

Lonny wasn't sure who had shot Iago. He had picked up the gun and ran down an alley. Shit, for all he knew Dalbert was dead too, or talking to the cops right now.

Lonny was no fool. He kept himself from running. Long way to go and thinking to do. Even if Dalbert was dead too, they'd find out the three of them had been friends. The doctor with the gun could identify him. And what about Reno, the drug dealer whose car they had stolen? He'd see the newspapers or the TV, see Iago's name, figure out who took his wheels, got him messed up with a cop shooting, and he'd be after Lonny too, maybe quicker than the cops.

There was a Burger King across Broadway. Lonny crossed, went in, bought three cheeseburgers and a Coke and sat down where he could see the door.

He had less than three dollars left and nowhere to go, but he had a gun and not much to lose.

Lonny watched the door, telling himself that the cops weren't going to come into every Taco Bell and Burger King, not for him, not for one black kid. He'd never seen cops doing that. There weren't enough cops. He had time, a little time.

He had to get out of the city. That's it. Out of the city, maybe to Atlanta, where his cousin Jackie lived. Tell nobody. Lonny shivered and chewed a dry burger, wondering what had happened to his saliva. Lonny had never been more than ten miles from the city limits of Chicago. Atlanta was as far as China, but he had to go, had to have some money. He'd call his mother, sister, tell them he was sorry, not tell them where he was going. Cops couldn't be there yet. Not yet. He had time. Not to go home, but to call.

Then he remembered Skilly Parker, the bar on Forty-second. Skilly was trying to sell his car. That was a week—no, two weeks ago. Skilly hung out at the Ease Inn Bar. He wanted three hundred for the car, cash, a '72

Chevy with the miles rolled back, had papers and everything.

Three hundred cash.

Lonny couldn't finish his second burger. He left it and the unwrapped one on the table and got up.

"Clean your trash," said a raggedy old white lady with a shopping bag on the table in front of her.

Lonny ignored her and went for the door. Shit, what did he have to lose? He had a gun. He had to get out of town. He needed money.

The rain was coming down again before he got a block from the Burger King. It wasn't much of a rain, but Lonny had a lot of walking to do in it. He pulled up the collar of his jacket and decided he would hold up the grocery store near the hospital, a little convenience stop for doctors, nurses, and clean-up people. Carryouts, some fruit, hot coffee. It was home turf. There were places to hide when he was done till he could move out of the city.

Lonny stopped at an outdoor phone booth, found a quarter, and looked up the number of the Ease Inn. About half of the pages were missing from the phone book, torn out. The right page of Es was still intact. A good sign. He dropped the quarter in the slot and hit the buttons.

"Ease Inn," came a man's voice.

"Skilly there?" asked Lonny.

"He's here. I'll get him."

Lonny looked up and down the street, shifting his weight from one leg to the other. There weren't many black people around here but there were some inside the stores and restaurants he had passed.

"Skilly here," came a nervous voice.

"Lonny, Lonny Wayne. Say, man, you still tryin' to sell the ol' Chevy?"

"Still tryin'," Skilly said. "You buyin'?"

"How long you gonna be there?"

"Till you get here with three hundred bills, cash money."

"What time's it now?"

"Little after one by the Bud Light clock over Howard's head," said Skilly.

Lonny thought quickly. Shit. He'd take a chance on the subway, pick it up on Chicago Avenue.

"I'll be there with cash by four," Lonny said. "You have the car and the papers."

"Will be," said Skilly and hung up.

Lonny was wet and cold. He plunged his hands into his pockets and hurried down the street, covering the precious bouncing weapon to protect it from the rain.

A long walk and a short subway ride without incident and Lonny Wayne was back on his turf.

He arrived thirty minutes after the three black men with Spanish accents who were making the rounds of hangouts, bars, and fast-food joints looking for a brother named Lonny with a dark lightning scar through his right eyebrow.

Lieberman's eyes moved from Rozier to Betty Franklin and stayed with her. He had the feeling that if she had not stopped Harvey Rozier when he came into the living room and Rozier had not seen Lieberman, something . . . Lieberman knew the look of nervous guilt, but it wasn't on the face of Harvey Rozier. It belonged to Betty Franklin, who stood a few feet from Rozier, trying not to meet Lieberman's steady brown eyes.

Rozier and Betty Franklin? She was old enough to be his mother, and Rozier's murdered wife had been a beauty— not that Betty Franklin was a *meeskite*, but still . . . Kenneth Franklin was a dying man, a rich dying man. A motive definitely suggested itself.

"A few questions," Lieberman said, standing. "You must have the funeral to arrange, all kinds of things. I remember when my mother died. Had to take care of everything. My brother and me. My father was already gone."

"I appreciate your empathy," said Rozier. "If Dana's body is released by the medical examiner and can be . . . prepared by the funeral home, the funeral will be tomorrow."

Betty Franklin's eyes had closed when Harvey Rozier spoke. She wrung her hands, actually wrung her hands.

Lieberman couldn't remember seeing someone do that since Mary Astor in the *The Maltese Falcon*.

"I gotta tell you this," Lieberman said, scratching his head and smiling. "My mother, can you imagine this, a widow for ten years, a woman almost seventy years old, has a heart attack in the tub where she's taking a bath with the son of my father's partner, Bernie Witt. Bernie couldn't have been more than . . ." Lieberman looked at Rozier now and continued, "your age."

The result was more and better than Lieberman had expected.

Betty Franklin looked as if she were going to collapse. She caught her breath and moved to the nearby table for the comfort of a cigarette.

"Can we come to the point, Detective?" Rozier said, being careful, Lieberman was sure, not to look at Betty Franklin, who was fumbling with a lighter.

"Sorry," said Lieberman. "Long night. Hard day. Family problems."

"I would like to get to my office," Rozier said.

"One or two questions and . . ." Lieberman opened his hands, "I'm on my way."

"Do you mind if Mrs. Franklin goes in the other room while we finish talking?" Rozier said. "I think she's been upset enough by the last two days—"

"But it's Mrs. Franklin I want to talk to," said Lieberman.

Betty Franklin almost dropped the lighter she was about to use.

"Me?" she said, looking at Harvey, who still avoided her eyes.

"I'm sorry to say this," Lieberman said, looking deeply pained as he sat back down, hands folded in his lap. The chair may have been an antique, but it wasn't comfortable. Still, Lieberman did his best to look as if he would be content to sit there for hours. "But my partner, Hanrahan—" Lieberman shook his head. "He thinks Mr. Rozier is somehow involved in what happened to his wife. Or at least that he knows something."

"Your captain told me—" Rozier began with indignation as Betty Franklin managed to make it to a chair, where she sat with perfect posture, an unlit cigarette in her hand.

"And your complaint was heeded. Bill's been reprimanded, but ... he won't stop, and I'm afraid Captain Kearney's told him to make some more inquiries. To stay away from you, mind you, but to make more inquiries."

"This is crazy," Rozier said, taking a quick glance at Betty Franklin to see how she was holding up. "I think I'll ask you to leave now, Lieberman."

"Suit yourself," Lieberman said, rising from the chair. "Mrs. Franklin, could you accompany me to the station for a few questions?"

A definite gasp escaped from Betty Franklin.

"Hold it," said Rozier, stepping in front of Lieberman angrily. "She's not leaving here or answering any questions till I talk to Ken. Are you crazy, Lieberman?"

"I'm the cop you requested, remember?" Lieberman said. "I think we should get some answers, give them to Hanrahan and Kearney, and show them that you couldn't possibly be involved."

"It's horrible," Betty Franklin said with a shudder.

"Horrible," Lieberman agreed with a sympathetic sigh.

"A man's wife is murdered, and he is immediately suspected," Rozier said. "Is that the way it's done?"

"Usually," said Lieberman. "Or when the husband dies, the wife is suspected. It's stupid, simpleminded, shows a lack of imagination on the part of the police, but you'd be amazed at how often it turns out to be true. Not this time, of course. You've been cooperative, helpful. I told the captain, but—"

"Detective, please stop babbling and ask your questions," Betty Franklin said, her voice low, just within control.

"I really don't think—" Rozier began.

"You were sitting next to Mr. Rozier all through the concert?" Lieberman asked, stepping between Rozier and Betty Franklin.

"I could see him the entire time," she said, looking at Rozier, who stood with his fists clenched.

"That wasn't my question," said Lieberman. "Were you sitting next to him?"

"We had seats together. Dana, Harvey, Ken, and I," she went on. "And . . . because Dana had been ill, Harvey insisted on sitting in the back, where he could step out and phone her, check on her. You know?"

"And you spent the entire concert looking . . . how many rows back?"

"I don't know. Eight, ten," she said.

"You spent the entire concert with your head turned, looking at Mr. Rozier?"

"Not the entire concert," she admitted. "But frequently. We, Ken and I, were concerned."

She was working hard at not meeting Rozier's eyes now.

"Enough, Lieberman," Rozier said behind him, but Lieberman went on.

"Are the lights on during the concert?" he asked.

"On stage, yes. The room is not completely dark, but the lights are down."

"My partner is there right now," Lieberman lied, just as he had lied about his mother in the bath. "He's having them turn the lights down to concert level and someone is going to sit in the seat where Mr. Rozier was sitting and my partner is going to sit where you and Mr. Franklin were sitting. What do you think he'll see?"

"I . . . I," she stammered.

"Lieberman, I was at the concert, goddamn it. I remember everything about the performance, every nuance, every slip. I'll never forget a second of it. It's a nightmare I'll always have. I should have been home with Dana. I should—"

Lieberman turned completely around now to face Rozier as Betty Franklin rose to take Harvey's hand. Harvey Rozier's eyes met those of Abe Lieberman and Harvey could see that the detective was no longer buying any of this or trying hard to pretend that he did.

"My partner's a suspicious man," said Lieberman. "He's seen just about everything. You own a tape recorder, a small one you can carry around?"

"Tape recorder?" asked Rozier.

"A little one," said Lieberman, showing an approximate size with his hands.

"Everyone owns a tape recorder," said Rozier. "What are you trying to say?"

"Me?" Lieberman pointed to himself and looked at Mrs. Franklin. "Nothing. Bill thinks you could have taped the concert, listened to it later. Crazy idea. I said it was crazy. I said if you wanted to kill your wife, you'd hire someone to do it. But Bill, Bill says you wouldn't trust anyone, wouldn't put your life in anyone else's hands. I'm afraid my partner has as low opinion of you as you do of him."

"Get out, Lieberman," said Rozier. "Now."

"I'm going to have to insist that Mrs. Franklin come down to the station and sign a statement swearing that you were not out of her sight for more than twenty minutes. Simple as that and I'm out of your life. I'm telling you, Mr. Rozier, Captain Kearney won't let it go till she does."

"Lieberman, why the hell would I want to kill Dana?"

"Mrs. Franklin," Lieberman answered and let a beat fall before he went on. "Think before you answer. Was there a time of more than twenty minutes during which you could not swear Harvey Rozier was in that room? I'll be asking your husband the same question."

Rozier put his arm around Betty Franklin's shoulder.

"I don't know," she said with a sob. "I don't know. But Harvey didn't kill Dana, and he didn't have anyone paid to kill Dana. He wouldn't, couldn't . . ."

"Because he loved her," said Lieberman.

"He couldn't," she said, and Lieberman believed that she believed.

"I'm going to ask Kenneth Franklin to begin a suit against the Chicago Police Department, you and your partner, and the city of Chicago," Rozier said, pointing at Lieberman. "You've badgered me and my closest friends into a near breakdown."

"That's your right," said Lieberman, walking toward the front door.

"I will no longer talk to you or any member of the police

department without my attorney present," Rozier went on, helping Betty Franklin into a chair.

Lieberman left the Rozier house without another word.

He had found a possible motive but still lacked evidence.

There was a bed, a dresser, a table with two chairs, and an overstuffed chair in George Patniks's room. Hanrahan found the overstuffed chair surprisingly comfortable. He folded his hands on his lap and looked at George, who sat on the edge of the bed, without saying anything.

"What?" asked George.

Nothing from the cop.

"He didn't identify me," George said. "He couldn't. I didn't do anything."

"He?" said Hanrahan finally.

"Hey, I can read the newspaper, I can see the TV. The Rozier murder. The old cop asked me did I know Rozier. Two and two make four. He. Period. Simple."

Hanrahan nodded and looked around the room, stopping at the wrapped painting George had been going out the front door with.

"You're good," Hanrahan said. "Bit morbid for my taste, but you got control, style, good sense of color."

"You know something about painting?" George asked suspiciously.

"Ex-wife did some painting," explained Hanrahan. "I read some books, took an extension course through DePaul, tried to keep up with her."

"Tried?"

"She left me."

"Sorry."

"Happens to a lot of cops," Hanrahan said. "Your mother always keep the television that loud?"

"Always," said George.

"Must drive you crazy," said Hanrahan sympathetically.

"I get used to it. Tell her to turn it down sometimes."

"I got a problem, George," Hanrahan said, looking around to be sure no one was about to leap out of a closet and hear the revelation. "Want to hear?"

"I guess."

"Got a woman I want to marry, but her people think I wouldn't be good for her. You want to know why?"

George shrugged.

"I have a reputation for sudden fits of violence," he said, shaking his head as if he had confessed to bearing a rare disease.

"Wait—" George said, getting up from the bed.

"You were going to skip town, break parole," said Hanrahan, still seated.

"I was going to check it out with my parole officer. I told you," George whined.

"Bag packed, painting wrapped up under your arm. Counting on an affirmative answer, weren't you?" said Hanrahan.

"I guess. She's been OK with it in the past for shows. I tell her how to reach me, check in."

Hanrahan was shaking his head no.

"What?"

"Rozier knows you, Pitty-Pitty. I was sitting behind that mirror watching his face. He knows you. The way my captain figures it, Harvey Rozier hired you to kill his wife."

"Never," George said indignantly, looking around the empty room for someone to believe him.

"Looks that way to the captain. I gotta see his point, you know?"

"I never hurt no one. My whole life."

"You got nailed for carrying," Hanrahan reminded him.

"I was a kid," George pleaded.

"Pitty-Pitty, I think I'm going to lose my temper. I can feel my Irish coming up on me," said Hanrahan, hearing his father's words, his father's voice.

"I swear on my mother upstairs," George said, hand to his heart. "I swear to the Father, Son, and Holy Ghost, to the Virgin Mary. I didn't kill that woman."

"I'm a Catholic, Pitty-Pitty," Hanrahan said so softly that George could barely hear him. "Don't lie in the name of the Lord."

"I'm not lyin'. I . . ."

"And you'll swear in the name of the Holy Virgin that you don't know who killed Dana Rozier?"

George stood silent.

"I think you're gonna go down for it, Pitty-Pitty. I think old Harvey Rozier is going to decide one morning that he made a mistake, that he suddenly remembers you. Your word against his and your word's not worth a tinker's damn."

George walked to the wall near the window, put his palms to the cool brick, let his head drop, and then turned around.

"What's the charge for witnessing a murder and not reporting it right away?"

"Don't know. Could be lots of reasons for not reporting a crime right away. Fear. Say a man has a record. Police can be very generous with an honest witness, even if he is a little late."

"Walk free?" he asked.

"Could be arranged," said Hanrahan.

"I saw Rozier murder his wife. You protect me from him. I walk and I'll testify."

"Still your word against his, George."

"Let me show you somethin'," George said.

He moved to the wrapped painting and began to tear away the brown paper.

Tricks and Traps

"Doctor Berry," Detective Applegate said, and Jacob Berry looked up from the waiting room chair at the policeman.

The waiting room at Edgewater Hospital still smelled faintly of cigarettes, though it had been a smoke-free room for almost a full year. Coffee was brewing in a corner. Newspapers were neatly stacked on tables. There were two others in the post-op waiting room besides Jacob Berry and his brother, who sat next to him. There was a pretty young Hispanic woman sitting upright near the bank of windows, an open book in her lap, and an older woman in a pink volunteer's smock.

The older woman, who had almost pink hair, asked in a whisper if either of the two detectives wanted coffee or a sweet roll.

"No, thanks," said Acardo at Applegate's side.

The Berry brothers were almost twins—same height, weight, glasses—though Isaac Berry was a good ten years older, hair fuller, with definite gray in his sideburns and a tired look in his eyes. The detectives, in contrast, looked nothing alike. Applegate was tall, black, bespectacled, and wearing a neatly pressed navy blue suit with a perfectly matched red-and-blue striped tie. Acardo, his partner, was short, white, almost bald, and definitely disheveled. They were known on the streets and in the squad room as Black and White.

Jacob Berry recognized the white officer. Berry had given Acardo a physical about two months earlier. Acardo should have been a physical disaster. He overate the wrong foods, got no exercise, and was on the verge of a serious drinking problem. His vital signs, however, were fine. No high or low blood pressure, cholesterol well within reasonable bounds.

"Yes," said Jacob.

"We'd like a description from you of the man who got away," said Applegate. "Do you think you could help us?"

"I . . . about six one, dark, wearing a denim . . . no, a leather jack . . . I'm not sure. He had a scar. Here."

Jacob made a slashing motion down his forehead through his right eye.

"Dark scar. I'd say it was at least a year old, maybe more."

"Anything else?" Applegate asked politely.

"I think he was the leader," Jacob said.

"Officer Matthews," asked the other Dr. Berry. "Is he, do you know . . . ?"

"Critical, but alive," said Applegate. "Bullet went through a rib and right lung, took a turn, and hit the spleen."

"I shot him," Jacob said, looking from one policeman to the other.

"Jake," his brother said. "I don't think you should say any more."

"According to the paramedics, you also saved his life in the ambulance," said Acardo.

"Thank God," said Isaac Berry, patting his brother's hand.

"Sorry to do this, Doctor," Applegate said, "but we've got to read you your rights."

"Wait a minute . . ." Isaac Berry said, rising from the vinyl seat that whooshed as he left it.

"No," his brother countered.

"They would have killed my brother if he didn't have that gun," Isaac insisted.

"Officer Matthews disrupted the robbery, not Dr. Berry," said Applegate evenly. "We're not really here to argue the merits of the charges, just to deliver them."

Acardo droned off the Miranda while Isaac Berry did his best to look angry and the still-seated Jacob Berry looked through the window over the shoulder of the pretty Hispanic woman.

"Possession and firing of an illegal weapon," Applegate said. "Assault with said weapon. Assault—"

"Wait," said Isaac. "Assault with a deadly weapon?"

"Charge has been brought by one Albert Davis, one of the three men who entered your brother's office this morning. He claims he was unarmed and Dr. Berry shot him. My guess is that Officer Matthews shot him, but we'll see when they finish getting the bullet out of Davis's leg."

"This is crazy," said Isaac Berry, raising his voice. "A man comes into my brother's officer to rob and maybe kill him. The man gets shot and he wants Jacob to . . . He can't do that."

"I'm afraid he can," said Applegate. "Was he unarmed, Dr. Berry?"

"Don't answer him, Jacob," Isaac said.

"The little one with the crazy face had the gun," said Jacob dully. "One of them, I can't remember which, had a . . . the heavy one—he had the knife."

"You sure?" asked Acardo.

"I'm sure."

"You're going to have to come to the station with us, Doc," said Acardo, looking at both doctors to be sure there would be no trouble.

"Fine," said Jacob, rising slowly with Applegate's help.

"Jake, don't say anything more, not a word. I'll have a lawyer at the station as fast as I can."

"I think we should go now, Doctor," Applegate said gently.

"This is illegal, a clear violation of my brother's rights," Isaac insisted.

"No, sir," said Applegate. "It may not seem fair to you, but it's perfectly legal."

"How would you know? Are you a lawyer?" Isaac said, stepping between the detectives and the exit to the waiting room.

"Yes, he is," said Acardo.

"DePaul University Law School, nineteen-eighty-four,"

said Applegate. "Now, I know you're distraught, but if you even touch one of us, you will be obstructing justice and we'll have to fill out a lot of papers and this could get very complicated."

"Isaac, please. It'll be all right," Jacob Berry said, touching his brother's arm.

"Oh, Jake, what'd I do? I talked you into coming to this goddamn city and now . . ."

"I'll be all right," Jacob said, moving toward the door with the two policemen. "The officer's not dead. He saved my life and I shot him. Can you imagine?"

Jacob's eyes met those of the pretty Hispanic woman. He thought she was, indeed, trying to imagine, and a look crossed her impassive face that made it clear that her imagination matched his deed.

Applegate and Acardo flanked Jacob Berry and ushered him down the blue-carpeted corridor.

It was Applegate's opinion, shared only with his partner and based on almost fifteen years of experience, that Dr. Jacob Berry would be a bigger television news splash than the Dana Rozier murder. Public indignation, the fear of invading blacks, and the gun control flap would make Dr. Berry a hero or a martyr. The sagging man between him and Acardo would probably walk away from all of this with a suspended sentence and a fine. The American Medical Association would probably issue a note of censure, but that wouldn't keep Berry from practicing. He'd have to leave the city, but Acardo doubted if at this point that meant very much to the young doctor. Applegate and Acardo had seen it before. Slightly different script, but same story. They could save a lot of time and taxpayers' dollars by packing Dr. Jacob Berry's things and putting him on the next train to Lordsburg. But that wasn't the way things worked.

"We're stopping for a coffee on the way back," said Acardo. "You want one?"

They stepped into the empty hospital elevator.

"I don't know," said Jacob, looking at Applegate. "I don't know."

* * *

Lonny stood in the parking lot and looked at the entrance to the convenience store. An ad for Virginia Slims showing a lean, light-skinned black girl with the whitest teeth and the fullest lips in the world glared at him from the store's stone wall. Next to it was a sign that announced a dollar off on a six-pack of Coke.

Lonny didn't try to find shelter. He was soaked through and tired. He just stood behind a car and waited till there were no customers inside. Then he looked around to see if anyone was heading toward the store before he hurried across the lot and opened the door.

The whole day had been a bad dream. It was just continuing. Lonny Wayne did not carry guns. Lonny Wayne did not rob stores. Lonny Wayne didn't get drug dealers angry with him by stealing their wheels. Lonny Wayne just wanted a few dollars in his pocket, a car, and the girl he'd met last night in McDonald's. What was her name? He had it written down on a sheet in his wallet. His ambitions were small. He wasn't even asking for the fox in the Virginia Slims ad.

Lonny grabbed something from a shelf, some Dolly Madison cupcakes. He brought them to the counter, where one of those people from India or somewhere stood waiting, watching Lonny drip on the floor.

"Anything else?" the thin, dark man said.

Lonny put the cupcakes on the counter and pulled his few dollars from his pocket. The man behind the counter, who had seen derelicts and addicts, robbers, and madmen and women in his four years in the store, was suspicious, but dozens with Lonny's vacant look came in every day. Money was money. The man opened the cash register to put in the two singles and give Lonny his change. Lonny saw bills in the tray. He had to be sure that there was a chance at the three hundred before he pulled this.

Satisfied, Lonny took the gun from his pocket and leveled it at the man.

"I have a wife, a mother, and three small children," the man said, as he had said the last two times he was robbed.

"I ain't no widow maker," Lonny said. "Just put bills on the table, fast. All the bills, under the tray too, and don't go pushing no buttons or buzzers or that shit, you understand?"

"Yes," the man said and began removing bills and laying them on the counter.

Gun in his left hand leveled at the frightened man, Lonny scooped bills and shoved them into his jacket pockets.

"You know who I am?"

"No," said the man.

"Good," said Lonny. "We keep it that way. You wait five minutes before you call the cops, you hear?"

"Yes," said the man.

"And you ever see me again you keep sayin' you don't know me, understand?"

Lonny was backing toward the door.

" 'Cause you ever ID me I'll get you or my friends will. You understand?"

"Yes," the man said again.

This is easy, and I'm good at it, Lonny thought. I get that car, head for Georgia, and do this again when I need cash. Me and Dalbert and Iago should have done this a long time ago.

He reached behind him for the door, and turned his head to look into the lot to be sure no one was coming. Far away in the hospital lot a man was running through the rain for his car.

And then Mohammed Achman Izar shot Lonny Wayne and ended Lonny's dream.

Lonny turned and fired at the storekeeper, but all he hit was the glass front of a dairy cabinet. Mohammed was a much better shot. He'd had more practice.

Lonny went through the door running, hearing an alarm behind him, dropping bills and hoping they were singles, wondering if there was a bullet in his head. He ran, ducked between cars, shoved the gun back in his pocket. Ran.

The forest of familiar high-rises, garbage bins, and traffic was a few blocks away. He ran, wondering if he would suddenly fall dead. Lonny panted, breathing hard. He slipped and went down, keeping his hand in his pocket to hold the bulge of bills. And then he was up again, hand to his ear. It came down with blood.

Lonny touched his scalp and couldn't find a hole.

"Everyone has a fuckin' gun," he panted, racing for the high-rises, the alarm behind him prodding him to exhaustion. "Iago, the doc, even the goddamn Indian."

He made it. The sound of the alarm behind him grew more faint. He made it. Between two dirt-gardened high-rises, behind an overflowing dumpster. Lonny leaned against a wall where he couldn't be seen, rain pelting, and in the eave of the dumpster he caught his breath and let his weary legs tremble as he counted the bills in his pocket. Two hundred and eighty-three dollars.

It would have to be enough for Skilly Parker.

Lonny touched his ear. It was bleeding, the part of it that was left. Lonny held his hand to his ear and looked around. He pressed his soaking sleeve to the wound and forced himself to move. He was alive. He still had a chance. But God, it had suddenly gotten awfully cold in Chicago.

They would follow him. Harvey Rozier was sure now that the police would follow him. But he would have to get away, have to go to Patniks's house, have to kill him—but more carefully, smarter than what he had done to Dana. He had made Dana's murder too complicated.

Lieberman was probably sitting outside waiting for him to come out and drive to work. Let him wait. Let him wonder. Harvey moved to the window, where he could see the driveway and street. Yes, a car was parked across the street, its motor idling. Exhaust fumes mixing with cold rain and turning to steam. Lieberman.

Harvey had managed to convince Betty Franklin that she needed to go home and rest. He had assured her with kisses that he loved her and that he had nothing, nothing to do with Dana's death. She believed because she wanted to believe, because it was necessary for her to believe.

Harvey crossed the bedroom and turned on the television. Images of war and soap operas skittered by, a cartoon about a dog, an old movie. He turned the television set off.

If Betty didn't believe him, if Betty abandoned him, he would have killed Dana for nothing. Ken had told Harvey that he had no more than six months or a year at best, and Betty had confirmed that one night in a bedroom at the Palmer House. Harvey had wept, and Betty had comforted her lover over the prospect of losing his closest friend, his confidant.

Rain hit the windows, thudded on the roof. Thunder rattled in the distance.

Dana was no saint, and their marriage had, at least for the past five years, been for show only. But, he had to admit, Dana had played her part well and she had been rewarded for it. She had never fought with him, had seldom even talked to him, which had been fine with Rozier. They had never discussed divorce. Harvey never could have afforded to pay her what she would have asked even if she had agreed, and he doubted that she would have agreed.

If he could have told Lieberman, Harvey would have said that it was she, Dana, who had repeatedly and openly been unfaithful, Dana who had picked up his friends, employees, and had even said that she was considering old Ken just to see how he would take the invitation.

The phone rang.

Harvey had been reasonably constant in his marriage.

The phone was still ringing. The answering machine clicked on, but the person calling didn't leave a message.

It was that suggestion by Dana that had set him thinking about Betty Franklin and the millions she would inherit when Ken died, not to mention the family money she already had.

Harvey did not believe in eternal life or eternal damnation. Harvey believed that whatever heaven or hell existed, it was on earth and one molded it or was its victim. They would all die. Ken sooner. Betty, perhaps with some subtle help, a little later, and Harvey last of all. If the police didn't catch him, there would be no punishment, only reward and the distant prospect of meaningless death.

The phone rang again. Harvey picked it up.

"Yes," said Harvey.

"This is Mr. Edgar, Mr. Rozier. I heard about your grief. I'm very sorry to trouble you now, but I need to pick up all that paperwork I left at your house during my visit the other day. You remember, the file where I caught that big mistake of yours? There's nothing for you to worry about now, but I'm leaving town and need to clear things up before I go."

Harvey sat and sucked in air.

"I'm afraid you can't come now," he said, reasonably certain, as his caller obviously was, that the police had tapped the phone.

"And I'm afraid I have to insist on getting it back before I go. In fact, I can't leave without it," the man said. "I didn't want to just drop by unannounced, so I'm calling you from the phone booth at the Shell station across from the church. I hope you understand."

"I think so," said Harvey. "I'll do what I can to help you out."

"Good," the man said, and hung up the phone.

Harvey moved to the bedroom window again. Lieberman, or whoever it was, was still out there. Betty would be back with Ken in an hour or two. Harvey had to hurry, had to hurry, and hoped he had understood the man's message.

Harvey moved to the closet, pulled out his sneakers, an old raincoat, and folded a pair of leather driving gloves into his pocket. Then he went downstairs, through the library and into the garage. Harvey had removed the red toolbox from the safe and it now sat openly on a shelf next to an aluminum toolbox. Harvey moved around his Lexus, opened the red toolbox, removed the small crowbar, and placed it inside the deep pocket of his raincoat. Then he opened the back door, checking to be sure it wasn't being watched. There was no reason for it to be watched, no reason for the police to think he would be running off, certainly not on foot.

Harvey pulled his collar up against the rain and hurried across the lawn and through a slight break in the bushes, the same route he had used just two nights ago when he murdered his wife. Through the wild, dead-end growth of trees and bushes, he wound his way, coming out on the cul-de-sac of Camino Real Road.

He leaped puddles and quickstepped down the street to the corner in front of the First Methodist Church. He crossed to the Shell station, looking both ways for Patniks. Nothing. Patniks had mentioned the phone. Harvey dodged through swishing traffic across the street and to the phone booth. The phone was ringing. Harvey picked it up.

"Hello," he said.

"I've got a problem, Mr. Rozier," Patniks said. "I've got to run. Cops came, put pressure on me, threatened, said they knew I knew something, offered me deals that were a crock of shit. I played along and went out my bathroom window. They're looking for me, Mr. Rozier, and if they catch me, I'm not going down for your wife's murder."

"I don't know what you're talking about, whoever you are, but if you know anything about my wife's murder, I think you should turn yourself in."

"I understand," said George. "But you understand me. I'm gonna have to leave my life behind, my mother, my work. I'm gonna have to break parole and run. How about you come get me? I'll think about turning myself in and talking about what I saw. You think about bringing ten thousand in cash. Animal barn in the Lincoln Park Zoo. Four o'clock. That gives you a few hours to get to the bank."

"I can't—" Harvey started, but George Patniks had hung up.

Harvey couldn't go home to get his car. He pulled out a quarter and called the Franklin house. Ken answered.

"Ken," Harvey said. "I've got to do some thinking. I'm going for a walk in the rain. You and Betty come over, let yourselves in. I'll be back before six."

"Well," said Franklin, "are you sure you want to be alone? Betty tells me that Liebowitz—"

"Lieberman," Harvey corrected.

"Liebowitz, Lieberman—a Jew name. What difference does it make? The man upset Betty, accused you—"

"He didn't accuse me, Ken," Harvey said. "He was careful not to accuse me. He said others were accusing me."

"Hearsay, clever," Franklin said with a sigh. "Those people are cunning. I have to deal with them more than you imagine, and they are cunning."

Harvey kept from responding to Franklin's prejudice. He had heard it before, disagreed with it, and made his disagreement known. Race, religion, belief meant nothing to Harvey Rozier. Everyone was equal. Everyone lived and died and was nothing. In the greater scheme of things, race and belief were small differences, not worth the extension of prejudice, the time and effort. A waste of time. Prejudice was stupid and unproductive.

"Just let yourselves in," Harvey said. "I'll be back by six. I promise."

"By six, Harvey," Ken emphasized like a concerned father hearing that his son might be home late from a date.

Harvey hung up and checked his wallet. A little under four hundred dollars. He called a cab and went into the station to wait.

He would have the cab drive him to Rush Street. From Rush Street he would jog to the zoo. Plenty of time.

At the zoo he would get George Patniks to go with him through the bushes to Harvey's supposedly parked car where the money and toolbox were in the trunk. In the bushes Harvey would beat George Patniks to death with his own crowbar.

Harvey didn't want the rain to stop. He wanted it to come down hard. A monsoon would have suited him, something that would keep people indoors and out of the park.

When the cab pulled into the Shell station, Harvey was outwardly calm, determined. He would keep it simple this time. Into the bushes, strike, throw the crowbar down a sewer, catch a cab back to the Shell station and home, free.

It could be done. It had to be done.

Circles and Confrontations

Three old men in baseball caps smoking cigars sat on rickety chairs under the awning of Uncle Will's Used Furniture. With nothing else to do but talk about old enemies and watch the rain, they watched Lonny Wayne swaying down the street muttering to himself.

"That there's a crazy boy," said Herbie McCallister, pointing his wet cigar at Lonny.

"That there's a street junkie, is all," answered Eddie Jackson. "Ain't you see 'nough of 'em to know? You gettin' shortchanged by the Lord in your old age?"

"Crazy boy," insisted Herbie as Lonny almost went into the curb.

"You both blind as snakes," said Little Whitney Styles, a near dwarf with thick glasses. "That boy's bleedin' from the head."

"No he ain't," said Herbie with contempt.

"I ain't lyin'. You'll see."

Lonny stumbled past them, and the three men went silent till he was a good twenty yards away, and even then they whispered.

"Bleedin' all right," said Eddie Jackson.

"Dispute ended," said Little Whitney. "Pay up, gents."

"You a damn fool or what?" asked Herbie. "Ain't no one bet with you."

"Herbie's right," echoed Eddie Jackson.

"He's goin' into the Ease Inn, look," said Little Whitney.

They looked, and Lonny Wayne pushed open the tavern door and staggered in, swallowed by darkness.

Rain and sweat and maybe a little blood were trickling

175

into Lonny's eyes as he tried to adjust to the near darkness. In the corner over the bar a guy on television was giving baseball scores and saying that games all over the Midwest were being canceled by rain.

"Man," a voice came from behind the bar. "You know you lost your ear? You're bleedin' all over my floor."

"Skilly Parker, you here?" Lonny said, making out shapes now, a shape at the bar, two or three shapes in one of the booths near the front.

Signs for Coors, Bud, and Swedish vodka were lit up over the bar. Photographs of boxers, all autographed, were taped to the mirror behind the bar. John Mogabi, Kid Gavilan, Randy Sandy, Joe Louis. The only one Lonny had heard of was Joe Louis, but he didn't know much about him other than he had been champ and had died crazy thinking the wop gangs were trying to kill him.

"Skilly," Lonny insisted, feeling heavy and dizzy. The smell of alcohol wasn't helping any.

"Here," called the bartender, and something hit Lonny.

He yelped and pulled out his gun.

"Hey, man, easy," the bartender said. "Just a towel to clean yourself and slow the bleeding. You can put the piece away."

Lonny could see better now. The bartender, Howard Caroline, who also owned the place, stood behind the bar. At the end of the bar sat Skilly Parker nursing a drink, wearing black pants and a black sweater, his hair konked back like an Uncle Tom. Skilly couldn't have been more than twenty.

"What's happenin', Lonny my man?" Skilly said brightly.

Lonny pressed the towel to his ear. First a stab of pain and then warm comfort.

"I got two hundred eighty-three dollars," said Lonny, walking toward Skilly, the gun at his side.

"No problem," Skilly said. "I can live with that."

Lonny was swaying in front of Skilly Parker now.

"Here's the key. Car's right outside around the corner," Skilly went on, pulling a lone key from his pocket and sliding it down the bar to Lonny, who almost missed it.

Skilly turned his eyes away from Lonny and examined the list of rain outs on the television.

"You want your money or you don't?" asked Lonny, confused.

"Just put it on the bar. Howard'll take out what I owe him and give me the rest. Car's full of gas. Needs oil every hundred fifty miles or about. Papers in the glove compartment."

"Take your keys and go, boy," Howard said. "Keep the towel."

Lonny tore bills out of his pocket and dropped them willy-nilly on the counter. He pocketed the key and began backing out of the Ease Inn when an arm came around his neck and he felt something press against his still-good ear.

"You got one ear left, man," the man behind him said with a Spanish accent. "You wanna keep it or you wanna look like the snake boy in the circus?"

Lonny tried to point his pistol over his shoulder into the face of the man behind him, but something hard and heavy hit his hand and the gun was torn away. In front of Lonny were two men. They were very black and very similar.

"Hombre," said the older of the two, "don't be an asshole. Put your hands down, keep what you got left of your eyes and your balls. You know what I'm saying?"

"Get him out of here," said Howard the bartender.

"We're goin'," said the man in front of Lonny, the one who had spoken.

The man behind Lonny holding a knife to his ear reached into Lonny's pocket, pulled out the car key, and threw it to Skilly Parker, who caught it in two hands.

"Lonny my man," said Skilly. "They didn't give me no choice."

Lonny Wayne began to cry.

The weather was with Harvey Rozier. It was raining, raining hard when he pulled the hood of his raincoat over his head and crossed Rush Street.

Lightning cracked. Thunder roared and Harvey's heart pounded as he put on his leather gloves as he moved and felt the crowbar bounce against his thigh through the raincoat.

Cabs and cars, their lights on, swished along the road along the west side of Lincoln Park near the zoo. Harvey hurried along, head covered, face in the shadow of his hood.

He could see the zoo barn up ahead, down the slope, through the trees. He could hear the cows inside mooing at the storm, could already smell the animals as he approached.

To his left toward Goethe Street just beyond the empty playground was a patch of bushes, not as thick as he had remembered, but they would have to do. Walking along the slope and partly covered by the trees, Harvey eased out the crowbar and carefully wiped it under his raincoat. His leather gloves squeaked against the iron. Rain clapped loudly off the leaves and the top of the barn.

Harvey moved at an angle to the open barn door toward the children's zoo and glanced back. There was someone in there. Just one person. He had been afraid that a family might have taken refuge from the rain, but the rain had been coming down hard most of the afternoon and anyone who had been trapped by it had taken their chances by now.

Harvey looked around quickly and hurried to the open barn door. George Patniks stood at the end of the short corridor of cow and horse pens. He stepped away from the nearest pen and put his hands in his pockets.

"Rozier?" he asked.

Rozier, a slick, dark green hooded specter, glided forward toward the obviously frightened man.

George took a step back. A horse kicked the ground nervously and the cows mooed madly.

"I've got the money," Harvey said softly.

"You won't hear from me again," said George. "I promise. This isn't the start of blackmail or anything. I just need enough to get away."

"You won't come back and you won't talk?" asked Rozier sincerely.

"What have I got to talk about?" George said.

"About what you saw in my kitchen."

"I'm willing to forget you killed her," George said.

"I don't know, George," Rozier said, moving another step toward the thief. "You saw me commit murder. Who knows what you might try to bargain for if you get picked up one night when you break into a house?"

"I wouldn't do that," George said, taking his hands from his pockets. "Why would I? How could I explain my not telling anyone before? I'd be an accessory. I swear. You're safe."

"I believe you," said Rozier with a sigh. "You can't blame me for being a little edgy."

"No," said George. "Look, how about you give me the money and the toolbox and I'm gone?"

"They're in the trunk of my car. Out on the street. You'll have to get a little wet, but the compensation is worth it."

"The trunk of your car?" asked George suspiciously. "I think maybe I'd rather just stay here and you go get it."

"Someone might walk in," said Rozier.

"I'll take the chance. Someone comes and we move somewhere else and make the deal."

"I don't think I want to take the chance, George," Rozier said, moving toward George.

Harvey was sure he was close enough to catch the thief if he turned and tried to run. He fingered the crowbar in his pocket through his tight glove and decided to move quickly, strike hard, be sure the thief was dead, drop the crowbar, rifle the man's pockets, and run into the rain. Worst case? Someone would see a man in a raincoat and hood running away from the zoo. The raincoat would go in the nearest trash bin and Harvey would walk to Rush Street and catch a cab before anyone had time to report the murder, even if they had witnessed it.

"Don't do this, Mr. Rozier," George pleaded, seeing the crowbar come out of Rozier's pocket.

The cows were bellowing now, and both horses were scraping their hooves against the cement under the hay in their pens.

"No choice, George," he said, ready to leap as George's

eyes darted around the barn looking for somewhere to jump.

Rozier stepped forward, crowbar over his head, as George tried to cover himself.

"He's gonna kill me," George screamed as a voice from the doorway called, "Harvey."

Harvey Rozier turned. Lieberman stood in the doorway, his hands in his coat pocket.

"You think you for Chrissake waited long enough?" George wept, his back pressed against the wooden wall, his breath coming in short spurts.

Rozier turned to George Patniks. Behind the thief in the only other entrance to the building stood Hanrahan and a uniformed cop in a slicker.

"This man killed Dana," Rozier said, pointing at Patniks. "He called me, said he wanted to turn himself in. I went crazy. I decided to come here and kill him."

"Drop the crowbar and we'll go someplace warm and dry and talk about it," said Lieberman.

Rozier turned to face the detective.

The animals were in a panic now.

"Believe me, Lieberman," Rozier said, pulling down his hood to show a sincere, grief-stricken face.

"We heard you talking to Mr. Patniks," Hanrahan said.

Rozier turned to face him. The policemen were moving toward him.

"Heard every word," said Lieberman.

"I didn't recognize him in the lineup because he changed the color of his hair," said Rozier. "His hair was red when he came to my door and he had a mustache."

"And you never let him in and you never hid his tool-box?" asked Hanrahan. "And you just confessed to murdering your wife to trap him?"

"Yes," said Rozier. "Yes."

"Well, we'll play the tape back," said Lieberman over the bellowing of the animals. "but I don't think anyone's going to believe it. Officer, read Mr. Rozier his rights and we'll take him somewhere where he can see some of

George's artwork. I think one painting will be particularly interesting to you."

As Hanrahan moved forward past George Patniks, the patrolman began to read Rozier his rights. Harvey could see the man's mouth moving but the cacophony of animal sounds and battering rain drowned him into vague sounds.

"I want my lawyer," said Rozier indignantly.

"No problem," said Lieberman, now only a few yards away. "You can call Mr. Franklin before we start talking at the station. We'll give him our evidence and have him listen to the tape and then we'll leave you alone to decide on your legal action. Unless you've got more to say before you talk to Mr. Franklin, all we have to add is that you are under arrest for the murder of Dana Louise Roberts Rozier."

Rozier started to raise the crowbar and took a step toward Lieberman. Lieberman took his hand out of his pocket and aimed his weapon at Rozier's stomach.

"It's noisy in here," Lieberman said loudly. "Just drop the crowbar now and we'll go somewhere quiet."

Rozier dropped the crowbar. The clank of iron against cement startled the animals into silence.

Evening Tides

Simon, the Franklins' favorite waiter in the dining room of the Winnetka Harbor Club, saw Ken coming and hurried to usher him to the table where his wife was waiting.

Ken Franklin was late.

At their usual table near the window overlooking the lake, Betty sat playing with a drink, probably Scotch and whatever she could think of. Her eyes were unfocused, staring into the darkness coming over the horizon.

"Sorry I'm late," Ken said as Simon held the chair out for him and he sat.

The crowd was light for a Friday night but it was still on the early side. A few tables away the Piries were already into their soup and beyond them Marjorie and Thomas Benson were entertaining an old woman Ken did not recognize.

Old, however, had become a relative term.

"I'll have—" Ken began.

"Mrs. Franklin has already ordered your drink," Simon said with a smile. "Vodka gimlet."

Ken nodded and examined his wife. Tired, shoulders bare and sagging, wearing Ken's favorite blue silk dress. Hair clean, white, and impeccable.

She looked at her husband, chewed on her lower lip for an instant and said, "What happened?"

There were bread sticks on the table. Ken took one, cracked it in half, and put it on the white tablecloth in front of him.

"I will not be representing Harvey on the criminal charges the state's attorney has brought against him."

"Oh," said Betty.

"Would you like to know why I will not be representing Harvey? There are four reasons."

"Yes," she said softly.

"First, the police have considerable evidence, including a taped conversation and an eyewitness. There are ways to deal with both and other, more circumstantial, evidence, but I am convinced that Harvey murdered Dana."

They went silent as Simon placed the vodka gimlet in front of Ken and waited for Ken to taste it. He did and nodded his approval. Only then did Simon place the menus before them.

"Would you like to order or would you like awhile longer?"

"Give us five minutes, would you, Simon?"

"Of course."

And Simon disappeared.

"Second," said Ken after a substantial drink from his glass, "I am sure whoever his attorney is, and I have recommended Lon Saunders, Harvey will plead not guilty. With delays and appeals if he is found guilty, the judicial process will take at least two years. As you know, it is unlikely that I will be alive in two years."

Betty said nothing but her eyes were definitely moist.

"Is that your first drink of the evening?" her husband asked.

"No, my third."

"The third reason I will not be defending Harvey is that you and I are certain to be called as witnesses by the prosecution."

"For the prosecution?" Betty asked.

"Yes. That brings us to the fourth reason I will not be defending Harvey. His motive. The police believe that Harvey killed Dana so that he could marry you when I die and have access to both my money and yours. Would you like another drink? I don't see anything in your glass but a very small cube."

"Yes, thank you," she said, and Ken turned to the waiting Simon halfway across the room. Ken pointed to his wife's empty glass and Simon nodded in understanding and moved toward the bar.

"Do you believe that?" Betty asked.

"Believe that Harvey would do that? Yes. Do I believe the obvious companion thought, that you and he have been having an affair, yes, but it doesn't matter. You will be questioned and you will have to testify under oath."

"I can't," she sobbed.

"We're going to have enough to deal with without you falling apart in public," he said, glancing toward the Bensons' table to see if they had observed Betty's loss of control. They hadn't or they were too polite to let it show. There were going to be many moments like this over the coming months.

"I'm sorry," she said, wiping her eyes as Simon approached with a fresh drink, placed it before her, and moved quickly away.

"Elizabeth," Ken said, "if my feelings were of real concern to you, you would have waited till I was gone to make a fool of yourself. Do you actually believe that Harvey Rozier is in love with you?"

"Yes," she said.

"Then there isn't anything more to say," Kenneth Franklin said, motioning to Simon, who glided to their table.

"Yes, Mr. Franklin."

"We'll both have the Norwegian salmon, broiled. And remind Andre that we like it with a crisp glaze. It was firm last time but not crisp."

"Of course," Simon said. "House salad?"

"Yes," said Ken, smiling at his wife across the table. "And Mrs. Franklin may want still another drink. She seems to have finished the one you just brought."

Chuculo Fernandez stood in the lobby of the Clark Street Station looking less like a man who was about to be free than a man who had been seriously wronged.

"Viejo," said El Perro, "Piedras is out in the car. You want to come out, say hello, somethin'?"

"No, give him my best," said Lieberman.

Piedras was a great, hulking, brainless creature with none of El Perro's affection for the old detective.

Officer Catherine Boyd was behind the desk writing something. Nestor Briggs had finished a double shift and gone home, at least for awhile. Odds were good that Nestor would wander back to the station in street clothes to talk to Catherine for awhile.

"Not much business tonight," El Perro observed, looking around.

"The rain," Lieberman explained. "Keeps people indoors. Drop in most crimes except murder. Murder, in bars, domestic, goes up when it rains. Keeps people indoors and irritable."

"No shit?" said El Perro. "You know that, Chuculo?"

Chuculo Fernandez nodded his head. El Perro's right hand shot out and slapped the young man's face, distorting it like an astronaut rocketing into space.

"Emiliano—" Lieberman said as Catherine Boyd looked up from her report.

"Chuculo should show some respect," El Perro said. "For you, for me."

Fernandez had cut at least six people Lieberman knew of and had almost surely killed two others. His eyes were stung and watering and he did not look as if he wanted to kill anyone.

"Despénseme," he said. "I'm sorry."

"Apology accepted," said Lieberman.

"I think maybe the rain's good for bingo," said El Perro. "What you think? Nothing to do but fuck, watch the TV, or go out and play bingo."

"It is beyond my expertise," said Lieberman.

"How come you never come to my bingo parlor? It's all legal."

"I know."

"You know, I figured something out," El Perro whispered, putting an arm around Lieberman's thin shoulders. "You don't need that B-I-N-G-O shit. You just like say *cinco*, five. You find a five someplace else besides under B and I have Chuculo eat your dirty underwear."

"The prospect of Chuculo eating my dirty underwear will probably lead me to a futile search for N-5."

"I don' know what the fuck you're talking about half the time, Viejo, but I like you. Hey, your *esposa*, she's the queen something of your church, right?"

"The president," Lieberman corrected.

"She wanna use my bingo parlor for to raise money for the church, I give you a free night and I call the numbers myself. No letters."

"I'll discuss it with her."

"Lieberman," said El Perro. "You're good like your word. You got something you need, another deal, you know where to find me."

"I know, Emiliano," said Lieberman.

"An' you, Chuculo," El Perro said, turning to Fernandez, who held his ground, expecting another slap or worse. "Maybe this will teach you not to fuck with no fuckin' little girls."

"Sí," Fernandez said.

"Let's go."

Both Lieberman and Chuculo Fernandez shared a feeling that Chuculo had a long night ahead of him.

"Drive carefully," Lieberman said as El Perro pushed Fernandez toward the door.

"Inside the speed limit, *siempre*," said El Perro and went out the front door with a laugh, saying to Fernandez, "You hear that? The man's got a sense of humor."

The death of Iago Simms and the wounding of Officer Guy Matthews belonged to Applegate and Acardo. They had taken delivery of Lonny Wayne from the Tentáculos, booked him, and read him his rights before taking him to the emergency room.

There would be another lineup later that night if Lonny Wayne wasn't hospitalized. Jacob Berry, who had already been released on bond, would sit behind the window and be asked to identify Lonny, who no longer looked like the Lonny who had attempted to rob him that morning. This was a one-eared Lonny Wayne, a much older Lonny Wayne.

It was almost six. The sun was going down fast. Lieberman called a good night to Catherine Boyd and hurried out the door. It was Shabbat, the Sabbath, and Lieberman was late. Maish and Yetta would be coming too, at least for dinner. Abe had invited Hanrahan to join him and his family and to bring Iris, but he had declined, saying he had someone he had to talk to.

It was still raining.

Hanrahan sat in the booth of the Black Moon Restaurant across from Iris Chen's father. Iris was waiting on tables and being careful not to glance at their booth. In the kitchen, Iris's uncle Chou, called out of retirement for the night, was cooking and frantically filling orders, all of which challenged his arthritic fingers.

"Look at it this way, Mr. Chen," Hanrahan said, hands folded on the table in front of him. "If Iris wants to marry me and doesn't, how is she going to feel? Who is she going to blame?"

Chen looked at him and allowed only an involuntary blink in reply.

"I don't drink anymore and I won't again. My divorce is final. I earn a good living, have a decent house, and I love Iris. Do you know what the other policemen call us? Iris and Irish? We've even got nicknames. A perfect couple."

Chen said nothing.

Dishes clanked. People at other tables talked. The kitchen door swung open and closed.

"I love her," Hanrahan said. "But she's not going to marry me unless you tell her it's all right."

"It is all right," Chen said finally, softly. "If Iris want, it is all right."

"I'll talk to Mr. Woo again," Hanrahan said, holding back a grin. "I'll explain."

"Don't need talk to Mr. Woo," said Chen.

"Listen," Hanrahan went on. "I know you're close to Mr. Woo and you don't want to upset him, but—"

Chen said something quickly, probably in Chinese.

"Mr. Woo don't like it, he can sit on the toilet with a monkey," Chen said. "It is something we say in Chinese."

"I'll remember," Hanrahan said.

"This is America, not China," Chen said, easing out of the booth. "You hungry?"

"Starving," said Hanrahan, smiling at Iris, who met his eyes across the room.

"We got special tonight," Chen said and hurried toward the kitchen. "You'll like."

Lieberman walked through his front door just before six-thirty and was met by his wife with, "Services are at eight. Maish and Yetta are late. We have to eat. You need a shave, and a lawyer named Seymour Greenblatt is sitting in the kitchen talking to Melisa and Barry. Put your gun in the drawer and get rid of Greenblatt. You can shave later."

He kissed her and she smiled. She was wearing the green dress, the one she had bought for her cousin Dorothy's daughter's wedding.

"You look great," he said, and meant it.

Beyond the living room Lieberman could see the dining room table set for seven.

"Lisa's not here yet either. Her car had a flat tire. Maish and Yetta are helping her fix it."

"The kids know about Lisa going to San Francisco without them?"

"They know. Barry asked if he could have his mother's room and Melisa said she didn't want to go to San Francisco in six months or ever because they gaze at you and give you AIDS," Bess said.

" 'They gaze at you and give you AIDS'?"

"Gays, Lieberman. She's smart but she's eight. You'd better talk to her."

Lieberman moved across the room, saying, "I'll talk to her. Maybe we should skip services tonight?"

"Lieberman," Bess said behind him. "I'm the president of the temple."

"What does the legendary Lawyer Greenblatt want?" asked Lieberman, moving toward the bedroom.

"To talk to us both."

"You brought the check back to Rabbi Nathanson?"

"I wanted it back in their hands today, so I handed it to his wife right after lunch," said Bess. "I'm going to check the food. Lieberman, a small helping of meat and no wine."

And Bess bustled off.

Lieberman took off his jacket and removed his holster and gun, putting them inside the night table drawer and locking the drawer with the key he wore around his neck. He wanted to shave but he wanted to have it out with Lawyer Greenblatt first.

When he opened the door to the kitchen, he found his grandchildren seated at the kitchen table looking at an overweight man with several strands of hair brushed over his bald head. In front of the man, who wore a sport jacket and suspenders, lay a briefcase amid the bowls of food.

The dinner smelled strong and full of garlic.

"Mr. Lieberman," Greenblatt said seriously.

"Mr. Greenblatt," Lieberman answered, leaning over to kiss Melisa's offered cheek.

Bess was standing at the sink, her arms folded.

"Your wife returned this check to my clients this afternoon," Greenblatt said, removing the check from his briefcase.

"Yes," said Lieberman.

Greenblatt nodded and returned exhibit A to the briefcase.

"This is a matter of great emotional distress," said Greenblatt. "Agreements violated, time and effort expended."

"Come to the point, please," said Lieberman. "My family is hungry and we're going to be late for services."

Beyond the kitchen door, the front door opened to the sound of voices. Maish, Yetta, and Lisa had arrived.

"All right," said Greenblatt. "My clients, the Nathansons, are willing to settle for five hundred dollars. With the five hundred dollars there would be an agreement that no more would be said about this unfortunate incident."

"I think you'd better leave, Mr. Greenblatt," Abe said. "You have anything to demand, you can call our lawyer."

Barry leaned forward, fascinated by his grandfather's anger.

"Mr. Lieberman," Seymour Greenblatt said, rising with some difficulty. "You misunderstand me."

"I'm not paying you a nickel," said Lieberman.

"No," said Greenblatt. "It is the Nathansons who are offering you five hundred dollars and their sincere apology."

Lieberman stood silent.

Bess stepped forward and said, "They want to give us five hundred dollars?"

"I have the check right here," Lawyer Greenblatt said, delving back into the briefcase to emerge with the check. "In return for which, you make no issue of Rabbi Nathanson's behavior. Ira hasn't been well. Lots of pressure. A move to get him removed as rabbi at B'nai Shalom. He's been going around giving thousand-dollar checks and trying to make deals on houses all over the neighborhood. Ira and I have been friends for years. All he needs is some time at peace."

"We won't bother them," said Bess. "And we don't want a check."

"Five hundred dollars," cried Melisa.

Lawyer Greenblatt opened the briefcase and solemnly returned the check to it.

"Thank you," he said, clicking the briefcase shut and holding out his pudgy right hand.

Lieberman shook it as the kitchen door opened and Maish poked his head in to say, "So, are we eating or what?"

"What are you doing for dinner, Lawyer Greenblatt?" Lieberman asked. "You're welcome to join us."

Greenblatt smiled and said, "Funny you should ask."

Laio Woo sat alone in the sanctuary of his seven-room apartment on Wentworth Avenue. There was not an item in the room that had not been imported from China. There was not an item in the room, with the possible exception of Mr. Woo himself and the black silk robe he wore, that was less than two hundred years old.

In front of Woo on a low, black enameled table, sat a vase, a colorful vase with the subtle narrow curve of a young woman. Painted on the vase was a garden and a young woman in the costume of a long-past dynasty.

This vase was but a copy of the original. This vase was no more than four or five hundred years old, but it was a good copy.

When he was a boy in Beijing, Laio Woo had first heard the tale of the woman in the vase, the trapped goddess who came out once every hundred years knowing that if she could keep from falling in love with a mortal, she would never have to return.

The goddess, however, was so giving that she always fell in love and each century left a grieving lover to return to the delicate vase.

A legend and only a legend, but Woo had devoted his life to the quiet search for the vase, the original, if it still existed. He would have given all he had for that vase, to touch the original, see the goddess before he died.

Laio Woo had been many things in his life—a poor beggar, a thief, a trafficker in stolen goods, and, on two occasions, the cause of the death of another human. He had also, for more than forty years, since she was a young girl, loved Iris Chen. Not the love that would want her in his home or bed, but the love of a mortal for a goddess on a vase.

Woo knew that reality would destroy his love as a careless sweep of the hand would destroy the vase before him.

And so he had watched her. And so he had seen her fall in love with a mortal, an unworthy white mortal. He could do more to stop their union. He could but he knew he would not.

He rose from his chair and lit a candle before the vase. Then he walked to the door and switched off the lights.

Laio Woo looked back at the vase and imagined that the goddess danced slowly, subtly in the flicker of the candle. He stood for more than five minutes watching and then left the room, closing the door gently behind him.

Four Women at Midnight

Kenneth Franklin snored gently and in the dim glow of the light from the illuminated clock face on the bedside table Betty could see the white face of her husband. He wore his white silk pajamas, and he lay without a blanket flat on his back, arms folded on his stomach. Snoring gently. Cheeks deep, sunken.

They had come home early, spoken little, and gone to bed without a "good night." All he had said was, "I've set the alarm for nine."

She wanted to hate him, but she couldn't. She knew she couldn't.

Her pillows were propped behind her and she was sitting up looking at him, unable to sleep, unwilling to get up and get a drink of water or wander through the house.

She would age quickly now. She knew that. Kenneth was withering even faster and determined to take her with him in his decay.

Betty pulled back the comforter that covered her. The novel she had forgotten on her lap tumbled to the floor with a flutter of pages. Ken didn't move and the gentle snore did not alter.

She didn't bother to search for her slippers. She moved quickly to the bathroom, closed the door, and looked at herself in the mirror. There were no lies here. Without makeup her defeat was clear, naked.

Slowly, carefully, though she was going nowhere, she opened the top vanity drawer and began to apply her makeup. She had to be able to face herself in the mirror.

After ten minutes, though she had no idea of how much

time had passed, the door opened behind her and in the mirror she saw the pale, white-clad figure of her husband.

"You closed the door. You know I need a light," he said and went back to bed.

No "What the hell are you doing?" No "Are you going somewhere in the middle of the night?"

Betty Franklin couldn't breathe and she couldn't finish and she knew she could not go back to bed and she could not wander through the house and she could not face herself in the mirror.

She wanted to scream, but the horror would be that Kenneth Franklin would have no response.

There was nothing she could do or wanted to do, and that was the greatest horror of all.

Wanda Skutnik stirred in her chair in front of the television on whose screen Greg Kinnear, who used to be on "Talk Soup," Wanda's all-time favorite show, was staring wide eyed at some movie star Wanda vaguely remembered. The movie star was young, dark, and beautiful.

The front door opened, slowly, carefully. Wanda closed her eyes. Footsteps on tiptoed stocking feet moved across the squeaking wooden floor. The television went off.

"Ma," George Patniks whispered. "You up?"

Wanda grunted and, eyes still closed, muttered, "Up, I'm up."

"Let's get you to bed. You shouldn't sleep in the chair. You'll get a sore back. You'll get ulcers or something."

He reached down to help his mother up but she didn't take his hand.

"Gregor," she said. "You're all right?"

"I'm all right," he said. "I'm tired. I'll be on the TV tomorrow. You'll find out. But I'm all right. No trouble."

"I thought the police . . ." she began and took his hand.

"I'm fine. No law trouble. A guy did something bad. I saw it. I'll have to testify is all."

With her son's help, Wanda sat up. She straightened her purple dress with her thick fingers and palms and looked at her son.

"You don't look good, Gregor. You want a snack? Corn Chex?"

"Just tired, Ma."

"You want to talk, Gregor?"

"Nothing to talk about," he said with a lopsided smile. "I'll take a shower, shave, and get a night's sleep. In the morning, you'll see, the old Gregor. Ma, what're you looking at me like that? You think I'm lying? Something?"

Wanda looked up at her son and smiled. It was a very small smile but it was enough.

"Oh shit," George said, looking away.

When he turned back to her, Wanda could see the tears in her son's eyes. He knelt in front of her. He had never done that before, never, even as a child. But now he knelt and put his head on his mother's lap. She stroked his moist hair and he said, "I can't go downstairs. I keep seeing her. I can't . . ."

"Sleep on the couch," Wanda said. "I'm not tired. I'll watch a rerun of a basketball game with no sound."

"I'm scared, Mom," he said as she stroked.

"I'm here," she said. "I'm here."

Charletta Wayne sat in the apartment window and looked out at the moonlight rubble that stretched below her across Thirty-eighth Street. It was a white and shadowed landscape, end of the world.

Her mother and father slept or pretended to sleep in the next room.

Charletta had come home less than an hour ago. She would have been home from the police station long before, but getting a cab to take her to this neighborhood was not easy and there was no way she could take the el this late at night.

Charletta had come home, kicked off her shoes, and sat in the chair by the window, not bothering to eat, not bothering to take off her dress, underwear, makeup.

She had talked to Lonny, talked to the police, talked to the man from the Public Defender's Office who represented her brother. Charletta's mother and father had refused to come. Her father's heart was bad. Her mother was humiliated. And so, as it always had, it fell on Charletta, the solid one, the smart one, the only person on either side of the family who had ever gone to college.

She had soothed her brother, talked rationally and reasonably with the public defender, who struck her as tired and a little stupid but well meaning. Lord, she thought, if you're out there among the rats and garbage, save us from the well-meaning and incompetent.

Something moved in the field and then stopped.

Tomorrow would be worse and it would be all up to Charletta, who stood tall and with dignity but no trace of beauty.

The Jewish policeman who looked like an old, tired dog had been patient with her, gone over the case against Lonny, told her what the doctors had done and that they were sure he would recover from his wounds and be all right.

"All right?" she said.

"Unfortunate choice of words," the policeman said. "He'll be physically fine."

"I'm sorry," Charletta said. "But . . ."

"No sorry involved here," the policeman said. "I'll get the lawyer from the Public Defender's Office to talk to you. Want some coffee, a sandwich?"

"No," she said.

They had been sitting in a waiting room at Cook County lockup.

"Miss Wayne," the old policeman said gently. "You've got enough suffering to do here. You don't have to be hungry while you do it. Coffee and a tuna on white? Place across the street is not awful. It's bad but not awful."

"How can I resist an offer like that?"

"I'm very persuasive," he said, rising. "Want anything in your coffee?"

"A little cream," she said.

He patted her hand and said he would be right back. And he sat with her till the public defender showed up, disheveled, tie knotted awkwardly.

And now she was back in her parents' apartment. She no longer thought of it as her home. It was the place of despair from which she was escaping. She saw the end of her brother. Jail, a record. Out in—what had the lawyer said?— four years with a plea bargain, maybe less. And then?

And she saw a threat to her education and future, her escape. She saw parents who needed her, an office job, receptionist, African-American with a white voice was always good for answering phones.

And she hated her brother, hated Lonny for being weak, for threatening her future.

"No," she whispered in darkness, determined, a little frightened, angry. "No, I'm not giving it up. I'm not going down."

From above a shrill crack of gunfire. She looked out the window. Something jumped and squirmed on a slab of concrete in the field below. A rat or cat.

Charletta shook her head.

"No," she said again. And she meant it.

"Lieberman, you're awake?"

"When am I asleep?" he answered.

Bess sat up and turned on the light. Abe looked at her.

"You want to talk?" she asked.

"I have a choice?"

"Yes," she said.

Lieberman sighed and sat up. "Talk," he said.

"What do you want to talk about?" she asked.

"I don't suppose you want to talk about the Cubs' chances at making the play-offs?"

"No."

"I didn't think so."

"Rabbi Wass gave a passable sermon, you think?"

"Passable," said Lieberman, holding back a yawn.

"I think if homosexuals want to join the congregation, they should be welcome," Bess said emphatically. "Jews are Jews. They're not going to hold hands or anything that Ida Katzman seems to be so worried about."

"Why won't they hold hands?" Lieberman asked. "You and I hold hands."

"You've got a point, Lieberman."

"Bottom line here," said Lieberman, "Ida Katzman, to whom I owe the pleasure of having been assigned to the Rozier murder, won't like it, and Ida's money is essential to keep the new temple in the black."

"I didn't say she wouldn't like it," said Bess. "But it sounded like she wouldn't like it to me."

"And to me too," agreed Lieberman.

"Want some orange juice?" Bess asked. "I can make a little popcorn in the microwave. That can't hurt you."

"Bess, I love you. You is my woman. You are a rare beauty who I love listening to and looking at. But when are you going to bring out the real agenda?"

She reached over and rapped the top of his head gently with her knuckles. He yawned.

"Lisa may never want to take the kids," she said. "She loves them, but . . . what do you think?"

"Never is a very long time," said Lieberman. "It's probably sufficient to say that she probably won't want to take the kids in my lifetime, which, if I avoid eating every food in the known world that has any taste, may not come till Barry and Melisa are adults."

"She's restless, Abe," said Bess.

"Give her thirty, forty years. She'll outgrow it," he said. "Popcorn sounds good."

"When we're finished," Bess said. "You don't mind, about taking the kids?"

"Of course I mind," said Lieberman. "What am I, Father Teresa? I mind. I mind that Lisa feels the way she does. That's what I mind. I'm worried about you and me having to take care of and maybe raise two kids at our age."

"But . . ." she prompted.

"All right. All right. All right. I'll get up and make the popcorn," he said. "The kids'll be hard, but it'll be good. There, I said it. You want an orange juice with the popcorn?"

Bess nodded yes and said, "A Thin Man movie started on AMC about fifteen minutes ago. You want to watch?"

Lieberman, in his pajamas, paused in the doorway.

"Popcorn, orange juice, Myrna Loy, and you in bed," he said. "Who could resist such an offer?"